HEARTS of AMISH COUNTRY

His PLAIN TRUTH

Gayle Roper

Annie's®
AnniesFiction.com

His Plain Truth
Copyright © 2018, 2024 Annie's.

All rights reserved. No part of this publication may be reproduced, stored in a retrieval system, or transmitted in any form or by any means—electronic, mechanical, photocopying, recording or otherwise—without the prior written permission of the publisher. The only exception is brief quotations in printed reviews. For information address Annie's, 306 East Parr Road, Berne, Indiana 46711-1138.

The characters and events in this book are fictional, and any resemblance to actual persons or events is coincidental.

Library of Congress-in-Publication Data
His Plain Truth/ by Gayle Roper
p. cm.
ISBN: 979-8-89253-183-2
I. Title
2018936934

AnniesFiction.com
(800) 282-6643
Hearts of Amish Country™
Series Creator: Shari Lohner
Series Editor: Jane Haertel

10 11 12 13 14 | Printed in China | 9 8 7 6 5

1

Aubrey Green watched the horse barreling toward her. Its eyes were wide with fear, its nostrils distended, its ears twitching. It threw its head back and tossed it from side to side. The young woman seated in a cart behind it struggled to hold things steady.

Aubrey tightened her hands on the wheel of her blue hatchback, a Kia Soul she'd bought back when she had money. In the five years she'd lived in New Jersey, she'd forgotten the dangers of driving on roads clogged with buggies and often nervous horses like the one she was about to pass. Coming back home to Honey Brook was reintroducing her to the phenomenon in short order.

She remembered her mother's words from years ago as she taught her to drive. "Be aware of the horses, Aubrey. You can't trust their reactions. Even the best-trained can spook if the circumstances are right. You are the one who can think. You are the one who must be in control."

Not that horses were stupid, but the point was clear: it might come down to human intelligence versus animal instinct.

Today she was fourth and last in a line of cars traveling this narrow winding road in eastern Pennsylvania's Amish country. She felt her shoulders grow tight as one by one the cars ahead of her passed the edgy animal and rounded the sharp curve ahead. She drew beside the horse, then the cart. She began to relax—another nervous horse passed successfully—when a motorcycle with a loud engine roared up behind her.

She glanced in her rearview mirror and saw a young man, the sun glinting off his shiny silver helmet, sending points of light skittering.

He was grinning broadly, clearly too intoxicated with the noise of his bike and the invigorating rush of air as he sped down the road to notice the horse, let alone its reaction to him.

The bike sent the already nervous horse over the edge.

The animal plunged off the road onto the grass verge in its attempt to escape the frightening noise. It compounded its agitation by running into the fine wire of an electric fence that corralled a herd of black-and-white dairy cows. The shock from the fence would have been minimal, but it was the tipping point for the horse. It reared in terror, its hooves pawing the air.

She automatically slowed and glanced back over her shoulder to see what was happening. The cart rocked and tilted as the shafts rose and fell with the agitated horse. Her breath caught as she foresaw disaster. If the cart went over, there would be no protection for the young woman seated in it.

The kid revved his engine with an extra-loud roar. Still grinning, he pulled out to pass Aubrey, coming even closer to the horse as he sailed over the centerline. With a casual wave of his hand, the boy and the bike disappeared around the bend, either unaware of or not caring about the catastrophe he'd caused.

Aubrey watched in the side mirror as the young woman jumped to the ground. She sighed in relief. The woman was all right.

Aubrey checked the road ahead—curve coming up fast—and slowed even more, then glanced in the mirror again. The horse was tossing its head and prancing in place. Instead of stepping back and being safe, the woman ran forward and attempted to grab the bridle. Aubrey caught her breath as hooves flashed.

I should help her. Not that she knew much about horses, but she could—what? Her mind was blank.

Without warning her car bucked and plunged in an imitation of the horse. The steering wheel jerked in her hands. She forgot the horse as she stomped hard on the brakes. "No!"

She had missed the curve, driven right off the road, and was now sitting at the edge of a field of knee-high corn. The car was tilted at an angle that couldn't be good.

With a shaking hand she turned the key to kill the motor. Tears stung her eyes. How could she have been so stupid? The last thing she needed was another crisis in a life littered with them.

She climbed from the car, knees weak, pulse thundering. She took several deep breaths, trying to calm herself. "Find three good things in the middle of the bad." That's what her mother always said she should do when bad things happened. It was supposed to make her feel better.

Good thing number one: she wasn't hurt. That was certainly good. Number two: the airbag hadn't deployed, which would have bruised her and left a powdery mess all over the inside of the car. Aubrey searched for a third good thing and gave up when the best she could come up with was that she didn't have to deal with an unhappy horse.

With a sigh she felt all the way to her toes, she started to walk around the car. It seemed undamaged. Maybe she could just reverse onto the road and drive off. That would certainly be a third good thing.

"You okay?" a male voice called from behind the car.

She turned to see a racing sulky pull up behind her, drawn by a large bay horse. She hadn't heard it approach, not even the clop of the hooves. An Amish man, his face ruddy beneath his straw hat, jumped down. "You okay?" he repeated even as he half turned toward the horse and cart.

"I'm fine." To her relief her voice didn't tremble as she'd expected it to. If she could just firm up her knees, she'd be great.

"Good. Back in a minute." With a wave he jogged toward the young woman, who was still attempting to calm her horse.

Aubrey watched as he approached them with his hand out. She could see his mouth moving though she couldn't hear what he was saying. She imagined he was making soothing sounds, because the horse's ears flicked in his direction and its agitation seemed to lessen.

In a short time, he had his hand on the bridle and was slowly pulling the horse away from the fence and back toward the road. The horse, ears cocked attentively, went with him without protest. When they stood on the grass but clear of the fence, he stroked the animal's muscled neck. The horse snorted and bobbed his head.

Relieved, Aubrey smiled. The man was an Amish horse whisperer.

He turned to the young woman, who wore a pretty coral dress and black apron. He spoke to her, and she shook her head, which was covered in the distinctive heart-shaped *Kapp* of the area. They talked a minute longer, and then she walked to the cart and climbed in. He continued to hold the bridle and soothe the horse.

Knowing they didn't need her help, Aubrey continued the circuit of her car. The front left tire was fine and the back tires were fine, all three on the grass verge. It was the fourth tire that explained the tilt to her car. It had rolled into a depression that had likely been carved by runoff after storms. The tire hung in midair, but that wasn't the problem. The problem was that it was damaged, a victim of a large rock it had argued with and lost.

Tears threatened anew, but she blinked them back. She refused to cry anymore. It was only a ruined tire, not a ruined life, though she knew enough about the latter to write a book.

She studied the tire. She knew in theory how to change it, but she'd never actually had to do it. That's why she belonged to AAA. Rather that was why she *used to* belong to AAA. In the chaos and cost of her move back home, she hadn't renewed her membership. Another thing to blame on Ethan Sharpe. She thought black thoughts about the man as she pulled her cell phone from her purse. Should she call one of her parents or her brother? Probably none of the above. They were all at work.

"Okay. Let's check your car."

Aubrey spun. The Amish man stood behind her. He wore the traditional white shirt and black broadfall trousers held up by black suspenders. His straw hat sat atop neatly barbered hair, and he had a sunburned nose in the middle of a handsome, clean-shaven face. She guessed he was in his late twenties or early thirties—a bit old for a man in the Amish culture to still be unmarried, as indicated by his lack of a beard. In other words, he was about her age, give or take a year or two, and single like her.

"The horse is all right?" She glanced over his shoulder to see it high-stepping down the road in the opposite direction.

The man followed her gaze. "He's fine. Scared but fine."

"I was scared too. I thought the cart would go over and take the young woman with it."

"I understand it was touch-and-go for a few minutes."

"It was the motorcycle."

"That's what Sally said."

"But the horse wasn't happy even before the bike came along."

"If I'd known she was going to take Peaceable, I'd have said no. He's too new to the road. Even without the bike coming along he'd be risky."

Aubrey knew buggy horses were often retired harness-track horses and had never experienced traffic before. Getting used to vehicles zooming past them took time and careful training.

The man examined her poor car. "So what happened here?"

"I was watching the horse rearing and the young woman trying to help him, and next thing I knew, here I was."

He made the same circuit of the car she had and stopped to stare at the damaged tire as she had.

"You have a spare?" he asked.

"One of those doughnut things."

"Good. That'll be easy."

She pressed her lips together. *That'd be easy if I knew what I was doing.*

"Pop the hood for me, will you?" He walked to the front of the car. "Let's make sure nothing's wrong there."

An Amish man familiar with an automobile? Maybe he'd spent his *Rumspringa* working in a garage. Or maybe he had a car of his own. She thought he was a bit old to be hiding an automobile in a cornfield, but one never knew. Maybe he rented a garage in town.

Aubrey climbed into the car and pulled the lever to release the hood. It really didn't matter how he knew about the inner workings of cars. She knew only the basics about them, so any help was welcome.

After a few minutes he called, "I don't see anything damaged in here. Can you turn the motor over?"

"I think." She slid the key into the ignition, and the car purred to life.

The relief that poured through her was immense. She needed this car for work. As a traveling physical therapist, losing her car would have meant losing her new job. Without that income, she wouldn't be able to pay her rent, her car payments, or her parents. Her savings were gone—another black mark against Ethan, the louse.

The Amish man slammed the hood closed. "I think your tire's the extent of your damage."

She switched off the engine and slid out, then walked around the car and stared at the damaged tire.

He gave her a lopsided grin and a raised eyebrow. "Let me guess. You don't know how to change a tire."

It wasn't said unkindly, but she felt her face flame. "I know the theory, but I've never had to do it in real life." When it came to cars she was more Lucy and Ethel than Wonder Woman.

"Let me move my horse to give you room to back up." He jogged to his horse, who was patiently standing, back leg cocked as he enjoyed a nice nap.

The young woman in the cart would have been better off with this animal rather than the clearly misnamed Peaceable.

As she climbed back into the car and put it in reverse, she couldn't help wondering about the sulky. Was it an Amish man's equivalent of a hot rod? Fast, racy, exciting?

Slowly she backed up until the car was level—or as level as a car with a bad tire could be.

The man walked to the back of her car and began hauling out the tools needed for changing tires. He pulled out the doughnut and rolled it to the front of the car, then returned to the hatch for the jack and lug wrench. "You'll need to replace this as soon as you can. By that I mean tonight or tomorrow. And don't drive too many miles on it."

He bent down, jacked up the car, and started removing lug nuts as if he did it every day. He glanced up at her as she stood watching him. "You should subscribe to AAA if you don't want to change tires. I might not come along next time."

She already felt stupid for driving off the road. The last thing she needed or wanted was a stranger telling her what she should do.

As if he'd heard her thought, he gave the most charming smile she'd seen in—well, she didn't know how long, but it felt like forever. "I'm Aaron Ropp by the way."

"Aubrey Green."

"Nice to meet you, Audrey."

"Aubrey."

"Right. That's what I said."

Aubrey, Audrey—it was a lifelong struggle to get people to hear her correctly, let alone spell her name correctly.

A few minutes later he stood. "There you go, Audrey."

"Aubrey. With a *b*."

He made a rumbling sound that could have meant anything.

What difference did it make what he called her? She'd never see him again.

2

Aubrey checked her watch. Only fifteen minutes late for her appointment at the Amish farm half a mile down the road. Glad she'd left early—and even more glad that Aaron had been on hand to rescue her—she drove quickly, thinking about the last few minutes.

Aaron was . . . interesting. He was handsome with dark hair and eyes, broad shoulders, and that charming smile, but it was his manner that struck her. She knew lots of Amish people. Her mother had been raised Amish, and Aubrey had grandparents, aunts and uncles, and cousins galore who were Amish. Because Mom had left the community before she joined the church, she wasn't shunned, so they kept close contact with her family. But even so, Mom was considered a bit suspect, as were her father, her brother, and Aubrey herself.

Aubrey had been thirteen when she overheard Aunt Maryann and Aunt Edna talking about her mother.

"It's because of religion," Aunt Edna said, her voice full of skepticism.

"Why else would she leave if it *wasn't* over religion?" Aunt Maryann asked as she peeled another of the two dozen hard-boiled eggs sitting in a bowl of ice water.

"Turner Green." Aunt Edna lowered each peeled egg carefully into the container of beet juice.

"But she hadn't met Turner yet when she decided to leave." Aunt Maryann scooped the shells into the trash.

"So she says."

"Edna." There was a touch of laughter in Aunt Maryann's voice. "You're terrible."

"I'm realistic."

Aubrey had tiptoed away before the aunts knew she was there. It was the first time she'd been aware of the speculations and suspicions that existed even among people who loved each other but lived different lives.

Aaron hadn't shown any of that cautious attitude. He'd talked to her without any guards in place. Maybe that was because he didn't see her as a threat to his family's commitment to Amish life. He neither knew nor cared who she was. Whatever the reason, he had been as at ease with her as any English man she'd met. Too bad he *wasn't* English.

Not that she was interested. Her battered emotions couldn't take the stress of a new relationship. Neither could her bank account.

Worried because she was late, Aubrey rounded another curve and found the farm lane she wanted. A sign by the road advertised a chicken barbecue every Friday night. Another advertised fresh strawberries. A shed sat at the end of the short drive, and through the open doors Aubrey could see baked goods and jams as well as the strawberries.

She glanced at the fenced area to her right. It was full of animals—hens, two miniature horses, a goat, a lamb, and a white turkey who spread his tail for her, revealing black feathers among the white. To the left of the drive was a garden full of vegetables with magenta petunias along the edge. The strawberry patch sat behind the garden, and two boys moved along the rows, picking the ripe fruit.

She pulled her car to a halt in the parking area by the shed and climbed out. Her clients were Mahlon and Miriam Eaby, who had been injured in a buggy-car accident. Mahlon had a broken femur, and Miriam a broken arm. Both had dealt with concussions, abrasions, and bruising, yet they'd been fortunate. A buggy made from wood and leather offered little to no protection in a quarrel with a car. Their horse had been killed.

She shuddered. What if Peaceable had headed into traffic instead of off the road? The girl, the kid on the motorcycle, or even she herself could have been badly hurt. There was a fourth thing she could be thankful for: the horse had veered right, not left.

A woman walked onto the porch of the big white farmhouse. She had her arm in a sling and still bore a few scratches on her face. Her hair was pulled back into a bun at the base of her skull and was covered by a Kapp. A little girl of about three, who appeared to be a miniature version of her mother, clung to her mother's skirts. A boy not much older—in black pants, suspenders, a white shirt, and a straw hat—swung himself onto the railing.

"Mrs. Eaby?" Aubrey walked toward the house, pulling her bag behind her. "I'm Aubrey Green. I believe you are expecting me?"

"We'd begun to think we misunderstood." Miriam Eaby smiled while her children continued to study Aubrey. "Please come in. My husband is waiting for you."

As Aubrey reached the steps to the porch, a familiar horse raced up the lane. She turned at the noise, and the sulky stopped beside her.

"Well, look who's come calling." Aaron gave her that charming smile once again, and Aubrey found herself smiling back. "Audrey, right? Didn't expect to see you again so soon. Or ever."

"Ever" was right. "It's Aubrey. With a *b*."

"Like I said." He gazed beyond her to the woman on the porch. "Hello, Miriam. Feeling any better today?"

Miriam gave a small smile, and her hand went to her cheek as if it still hurt to smile. She shrugged and grimaced. "A bit maybe."

"I'm glad to hear it. And Harper. How are you?" He winked at the little girl and she giggled. "Little Mahlon." The boy gave him a big grin.

With a final wave, Aaron shook the reins and drove to the barn, disappearing through its large door. Aubrey followed him with her eyes. *Such a nice guy. If only he wasn't Amish.* She reminded herself she was still in recovery mode. But if she wasn't, and he wasn't Amish? Well, who knew?

Aubrey followed Miriam, Harper, and little Mahlon into the house. The entire first floor consisted of one large room that served as living room, dining room, and kitchen. Aubrey had to bite back a smile at the idea that the Eaby house had that much-coveted open floor plan everyone wanted on the home renovation shows on cable. One thing was for sure—given the age of the house and the absence of a television, the floor plan was only modern by accident.

A windup baby swing sat next to a recliner in the living room area. A sleeping baby swayed gently back and forth beside her sleeping father, who reclined in a dark-green leather chair. A pair of crutches lay on the floor by the chair.

A boy smaller than the two children who had followed Miriam onto the porch sat in a portable playpen stacking blocks four or five high and knocking them down with a smile.

Four stepping-stones, Aubrey thought as she smiled at the children.

"I'm almost finished, *Mamm*." A girl, older than the four Aubrey had already seen but younger than the two boys picking strawberries, spoke to Miriam in Pennsylvania Dutch. She grabbed a dish towel and folded it neatly, then laid it on top of a high pile that wobbled. At her feet was a nearly empty clothes basket.

Miriam smiled at her daughter. "You'd better make two piles, Anna, or they're all going to end up on the floor and you'll have to start all over."

"Yes, Mamm." Anna studied her shaky clothes tower. With great care she took the top half and made a second pile. Then she cocked her head and smiled at Aubrey.

"I'm Aubrey. I'm here to help your mother and father get better." Aubrey spoke in Pennsylvania Dutch. She knew that the children, with the possible exception of the oldest three, did not yet speak English. They wouldn't learn their second language until they began school.

Four sets of eyes stared at her. The baby slept on.

"You speak Dutch?" Miriam said in English.

"I do." Aubrey smiled. "I have many Amish relatives."

"I see," Miriam said, apparently not quite certain what to make of that information. She must have known it meant someone had left the community and wondered if it was Aubrey and if she was shunned.

"My mother left many years ago, before she joined the church," Aubrey explained. "We still see her family regularly."

Miriam appeared thoughtful. Still, she seemed uncomfortable as she ran her hand over her younger daughter's head. "Would you mind speaking English around the children? It is less confusing for them, even if they don't understand."

What Miriam wasn't saying was that people like Aubrey, people dressed in slacks and a shirt with the Phoenix Physical Therapy logo, spoke English. People dressed like Miriam in a bishop-approved dress and apron and Kapp spoke Dutch.

Aubrey understood. "Of course. Would you tell me their names?"

"You know Anna." She indicated her little laundress. "This is little Mahlon." The climber of railings. "And Harper."

She had to wonder where Miriam had gotten the contemporary English name for the skirt hugger. Aubrey smiled at the girl, who promptly stuck her thumb in her mouth and hid her face in her mother's skirt.

"The one in the playpen is Joseph, and the baby is Naomi." Miriam gave her brood a loving smile. "Asa and Ben are outside."

"They're picking strawberries," little Mahlon said.

Aubrey smiled and said, "*Gutt.* I mean, good."

Miriam ignored Aubrey's slip. "I will wake Mahlon for you."

Aubrey held up her hand. "Let him sleep a bit longer. I'd like to see how you're coming along."

"I'm fine. Anna is my helper, and Sally Hoffman has come to stay for a while as our *Maud.* Our maid."

"I'm glad you have so much help." With all these kids, it would be needed.

"And Aaron has come to help Mahlon with the horses." She indicated her arm. "I cannot do much, either here in the house or in the barn."

"Nor should you."

Miriam closed her eyes and put a hand to her head.

"Headache?"

"A bit."

"A result of the concussion. It will pass." Aubrey indicated the straight-backed chairs around the kitchen table. "May we sit here?"

Miriam made a distressed sound. "Of course. Forgive me for being so rude. Since the accident I sometimes have trouble remembering things I should do."

Aubrey smiled her warmest smile as she pulled out a chair. "Be patient. It will be fine in a little while."

Miriam smiled as though she was unconvinced and took the chair next to Aubrey.

"Now let me see your hand." Aubrey reached for Miriam's injured arm, encased in a cast. She checked the fingers for any sign of blue nails, which would show an improper blood flow. To her relief, everything was rosy and healthy. "Wiggle your fingers for me."

Miriam complied.

"Can you touch each finger to your thumb?" Aubrey demonstrated.

Again Miriam did as asked.

"Let's do it with both hands." Aubrey touched her fingers to her thumb one at a time. Miriam followed suit. Out of the corner of her eye Aubrey saw Anna moving her hands, her face a mask of concentration as she mimicked Aubrey and her mother. Beside her Harper wiggled her fingers in some pattern only she understood. Little Mahlon studied Anna, then tried. He managed to touch his thumb to his index finger and his thumb to his middle finger. He frowned as he struggled with the other two fingers.

"Here's one we can all do." Aubrey opened and closed her hands, exaggerating the open part, spreading her fingers wide. Everyone followed her lead, and smiles bloomed on all their little faces.

By the time Aubrey left the house, she was in love with the Eabys. The father, Mahlon, was a small, energetic man who clearly hated being limited by his injury, but he was unfailingly pleasant, even when he struggled to do what would have been effortless before the accident.

She was smiling as she walked to her car.

"You like them," Aaron called as he came out of the barn, bridle in hand.

She told herself she wasn't glad he seemed to have been watching for her. "What's not to like? They're lovely."

He stopped beside her and glanced toward the house. "When I came, I wasn't certain they'd accept me, but they've been nothing but gracious and appreciative."

She couldn't imagine anyone not taking to a charmer like him. "Why wouldn't they accept you? They need you."

"They need someone, not necessarily me. When they sent to Iowa for help, they were taking a risk."

She thought of his handling the frightened horse with such ease. "You don't seem much of a risk."

He laughed. "I was to them. Think about it. Their farm. Their horses. And some unknown cousin who might or might not know what he's doing."

So he was Mahlon's cousin. "But you obviously do."

"They didn't know that. They'd never met me. They'd never met any of their Iowa relatives. Mahlon's uncle left this area years ago as a young man to search for land for his own farm and found it in the Amish community in Iowa."

Aubrey knew all about that. Large families and limited land presented a continuing challenge. Add to limited land an eighth-grade education, and many young Amish men had to choose construction or factory work to make a living. Mahlon was fortunate to have his own farm.

"But why did they send all the way to Iowa?" She couldn't imagine her own uncles allowing anyone in their districts to go unaided.

"Family is family, even family that is separated by many miles. That's the first reason. The second is that the need for help is long-term. It'll be quite a while before Mahlon's up to working with the horses again." Aaron shrugged. "It's an adventure for an Iowa farm boy."

Aubrey had to smile. "I guess it is. Did you fly?"

"On an airplane?" Aaron shook his head. "Bus is a lot cheaper."

"And a lot longer." She pulled her car door open and slid behind the wheel.

Aaron rested an arm on the roof of the car. "When do you come to see Miriam and Mahlon again?"

"Wednesday. I'll be coming three times a week, Monday, Wednesday, and Friday."

Aaron stepped back. "Nice. See you Wednesday, *Audrey*." He winked at her and gave her door a gentle push.

"Aubrey." The door clicked shut. "With a *b*."

3

Aaron took hold of Peaceable's bridle and held him while Sally climbed down from her cart. She'd returned mere minutes after Aubrey left. The horse tossed its head and tried to break Aaron's grip.

"You are one cranky beast today." Aaron tightened his fingers around the leather. "How did he do at the store?"

Sally glanced at Peaceable with dislike. "He complained the whole time I was there, shifting his weight, pulling against the reins at the hitching rail, snorting. He even nipped at the horse next to him, but the lead was too short for him to do much but catch air."

Aaron wasn't surprised. He was just grateful Sally had tied him short and tight. "When you need to go out again, check with me. I can tell you which horses are—"

"I know as much about the horses on this farm as you do, Aaron." She threw him a stormy expression and grabbed the bags from the back of the cart. "Neither of us has been here all that long. But I know what I'm doing around horses. The incident with Peaceable was a fluke. Besides, Jake said he was fine to take."

Jake Stoltzfus was Mahlon Eaby's assistant horse trainer. The man with the heavy hands, the thorn in Aaron's side. "You trust Jake?"

Sally shrugged. "He's been here longer than you or me."

True. Mahlon Eaby had hired him well before the accident. But there was something about him . . .

"Have you watched him with the horses?" Aaron asked.

"No. I'm a bit busy in the house. But I trust him."

"Why? Because he speaks your dialect and I don't?"

She looked startled. "Why wouldn't I trust him?"

Why indeed. Maybe because Jake was sneaky? Lazy? Chronically late? Slippery as an eel?

Aaron tried to swallow his frustration. "He did you no favor by suggesting you take Peaceable."

Sally glared. "You've been here, what? Three days? Four? Jake has worked here a year."

From what Aaron had heard, Jake had worked here less than six months.

"Who do you think I'll trust, Aaron? And wasn't Aaron in the Bible *second*-in-command to Moses?" As clearly he was second to Jake in her mind.

"I've seen Jake with the horses, Sally. Please keep your eyes open around him."

Sally gave a sniff and marched toward the house. Aaron watched her walk away. She wore a coral dress and black apron with her brown hair pulled back and tucked neatly under her Kapp. She was a local woman, stepping forward as a friend and neighbor to help in a time of need. He judged her to be about nineteen, old enough that she should be able to see through Jake's pretensions. She should be able to recognize the difference between that man's pride and swagger and Aaron's genuine concern and desire to help. Before today she had been pleasant if somewhat shy toward him. Before Peaceable. Before mention of Jake.

"Are you mad at me or the horse? Or yourself?" he called after her.

Sally stopped, frozen by his question. He studied her as he waited for her reply. Her lips were pressed together, her eyes narrowed. He couldn't tell if she was furious or thinking hard. He prayed for the latter.

Living here on a farm that was strange to both of them with people neither knew well—or in his case, at all—was somewhat awkward to begin with. If she chose to dislike or resent him, their stay would be needlessly unpleasant. Especially if she saw him and Jake as competitors and took Jake's side because he was local and knew their ways.

She took a deep breath. When she raised her eyes to him, she was still frowning, but he thought it was more in aggravation at herself than in anger at him. She sighed, her shoulders drooping as if the grocery bags dangling from her hands suddenly weighed her down. "It's not you."

"I'm glad."

She glared daggers at Peaceable. "The same cannot be said of you, horse."

The animal ignored her.

Sally rolled her eyes and stalked to the house.

Aaron shook his head at the horse. "You could at least try to be nice."

Peaceable snorted. Aaron patted his neck, taking care to stay well away from his mouth. "My my, what big teeth you have." And the horse did—huge, dangerous, and more than able to take a good-sized chunk out of whoever got in range.

Aaron led the horse into the barn and released him from the cart. Peaceable sighed in relief. With an understanding laugh, Aaron began brushing him down. "Hang in there. You'll get used to it."

The horse looked around, saw he wasn't where he wanted to be, and fell back into his moody funk. He fidgeted the whole time Aaron worked on him, shifting his weight, laying his ears flat, pawing the ground. Most horses liked being groomed—Aaron always thought of it as an equine spa treatment—but then Peaceable wasn't most horses.

"Easy, boy. It will be all right."

Peaceable tossed his head in disagreement. He clearly hated his new life.

He led the animal out the rear door to the pasture where two other horses grazed contentedly. One was the horse he'd had out when Peaceable was spooked. Mellow and calm, Meltdown would soon make a good buggy horse for some family, provided they didn't want to go anywhere too quickly. He was here because he hadn't wanted to go too quickly around the harness track either.

The other horse, Starry Night, would be fine eventually. He didn't yet like the noise and confusion of traffic, and it would be a while before he would be happy with the heavier weight of a buggy. Still he was intelligent and willing to work, obedient and strong. He had a pleasant disposition, a nice mix of spirit and the desire to please—the chief requirements of a family horse.

"There you go," Aaron murmured as he released Peaceable into the pasture. For that brief moment the horse seemed pleased at the freedom this patch of grass represented. He began to gallop the perimeter. Aaron closed the gate behind him, and it was as if that slight noise reminded the crotchety animal of his pique. With a shake of his head he stopped running and stalked to the far corner, where he stood with his back to the others, for all the world like a grouchy toddler who wasn't getting his way.

A soft whinny drew Aaron to the second pasture, where a chestnut mare and her colt made him smile. The colt was mere weeks old, all gangly legs and possibilities. He was dark with a broad white blaze down his face, and he hovered near his mother.

After watching them for a moment, Aaron went back into the barn to tackle his work. As usual Jake was invisible. Not that Aaron minded. It was better to have all the work dumped on him than to have to go around after Jake and redo everything he'd done sloppily or completely wrong. He couldn't for the life of him understand why Mahlon had hired the man.

Forget the slacker, he told himself. *Relax. Enjoy the rhythm of the work*. Aaron took a deep breath. This time here with the Eabys was exactly what he needed. The pressure at home to follow the prescribed path for his life was getting stronger by the day, and he felt like a boiler whose heat was building, with an explosion not far off.

He knew such an explosion would scald those he cared for and help no one, least of all himself. The weeks here would be his escape valve, allowing him time to simmer down, allowing the pressure to fade away, allowing him the perspective to solidify his choice. And to plan how to tell his father.

If only he didn't respect his father so much. The man was a paragon of character and the epitome of what a man should be. His work ethic was amazing and his abilities legendary. He met every challenge with determination and calm. And, like David of the Bible, he was a man after God's own heart.

But respect or not, amazing man or not, it was not his father's life. It was Aaron's. He must be the one making the choices, whether his father liked them or not.

"You know what you should do," his father had said just before Aaron had decided to take this job with Mahlon. "What you *must* do."

Aaron recognized the man's iron determination to get his way. Even paragons had flaws, and his father's was knowing what everyone should do. Always. The fact that he was usually right was beside the point. A man's life was all he had, and Aaron was determined to live his as he saw best.

But so often he felt he was snarling inside, aggravated at feeling pushed to do, to be what he did not want to do or be. He felt the way Peaceable must feel.

In the moment's frustration, he grabbed a bucket and swung it so hard the handle unhooked from the body. The bucket went sailing across the barn to smack into the far wall, then clattered to the ground.

Aaron went cold all over. What if one of the horses had been standing there? Even worse, what if it had been one of the children? He stood for a moment, eyes closed, chest heaving. *Oh, Lord, what am I becoming?*

He took a deep breath and walked to where the bucket lay on its side. He picked it up and reattached the handle, then made sure the horses had feed and fresh water awaiting them.

He wasn't used to being so filled with resentment and anger. Maybe his own stewing distress was why he'd spoken to Sally about *her* anger. He saw too much of it in himself, and the last thing he needed was to be around someone who was as prickly as she was. If he could draw the infection beginning in both of them to the surface to cleanse, they could live in peace. And he could be at peace with himself. Maybe he could even learn to like Jake.

He heard a car pull into the drive. He wiped his hands on his pants and started for the door. Could he be lucky enough for Aubrey to have come back for a second visit in one day? It was probably wrong of him, but he enjoyed teasing her. She was so cute when she was frustrated. He could always hope.

And hopes could always be dashed.

When he emerged from the barn, he recognized the black Mercedes convertible with its top down and the man climbing out of it. "Hey." He waved.

Trent Ingleston grinned at him. "How's it going?"

Aaron grinned back. "Pretty well."

"This is a nice farm. How are you doing with the horses?"

Aaron laughed. "Let me show you my biggest challenge."

The men walked to the pasture, and while Meltdown and Starry Night came to say hello, Peaceable continued to stand with his back to the world, tail twitching to show his displeasure.

Trent gave Meltdown and Starry Night a pat and fed them the carrots Aaron had handed him. He indicated Peaceable. "What's his problem?"

Aaron shrugged. "A grumpy nature."

"Where'd he come from?"

"I don't think Mahlon knows. He was at the New Holland auction, and he was too fine an animal to pass up, so Mahlon bought him."

Trent laughed. "And he doesn't appreciate his good fortune in coming here."

"He does not. Life made choices that changed his life without consulting him."

"Sort of like our fathers with us."

"Isn't that the truth." Aaron squinted against the sun and wished for Trent's sunglasses. "But we're not standing in the corner like crabby kids." He felt chagrined for a moment, remembering the bucket he'd just thrown. "At least not most days."

They moved to the other pasture, and Trent studied Adelaide and her colt. The colt made a circle around his mother, moving with the awkward yet beautiful joy of the very young. Adelaide nickered softly to keep him close to her. "Very nice. That little colt's a beauty."

Jake appeared for the first time in hours, standing with legs spread and arms crossed, the master surveying his domain. "He'll do, I guess."

Trent and Aaron exchanged glances. He'd more than "do." Anyone could see that. Aaron bit his tongue to keep from saying something he'd regret.

Jake turned his back on the horses. "That black convertible yours?" he asked Trent.

"Yep."

"Good mileage?"

"Decent."

"I'm thinking of getting one. You recommend it?"

"You're getting a car?" Trent sounded surprised, but no more than Aaron was.

"You think I can't because I'm Amish, right?" Jake stuck his chin in the air.

Trent ignored the challenge in Jake's voice and said mildly, "Well, yeah."

Jake laughed, a sly edge to his voice. "Rules were meant to be broken."

Trent studied Jake for a minute. "Why do you stay Amish if that's your attitude? Why not just become English? Then you can buy any car you want, though maybe not this one. It's pretty pricey."

"Oh, money's no object." Jake's whole manner screamed false bravado. "Everybody knows us Amish are rich."

Tales of Amish men buying farms with cash peeled from large rolls of bills had reached even Aaron. Somehow he didn't see Jake as one of those wealthy men. In fact Aaron thought he saw something in Jake he'd never noticed before—fear.

He played with that idea while Jake and Trent continued to talk. Had the fear always been there and he'd been too angry at Jake to see it? What did Jake fear? Life itself? Or was it Trent's question about becoming English that had brought the fear to the surface?

That must be it. Jake might mock Amish life, but it was safe there. He knew what to expect. He might threaten to leave the community or do something bad enough to be told to leave, but the thought of actually leaving probably terrified him. He was fine as long as he postured and scoffed, but Trent's question, asked with genuine curiosity—well, that frightened him. He knew he had no clue how to fit into the English world. He had too little education. He didn't know how to maneuver socially. In spite of his big talk about getting a car, he probably didn't have a driver's license. Maybe not even a bank account.

Aaron could almost feel sorry for the man. If he didn't come to his senses, he would probably fail at everything he tried, disappoint everyone he knew. He would make some woman a terrible husband and their children a dangerous father, exerting his power the one place he could.

Aaron studied Jake with his new insight. It didn't excuse Jake's poor performance or give him a pass on jobs not done, but it moved Aaron to be more encouraging to the man. Maybe he could even help him somehow.

"So I'm planning on buying the farm down the road," Jake was saying when Aaron tuned back in to the conversation. "You want to invest a few thousand? I'll make you a fortune."

Maybe Jake was a bigger project than Aaron wanted to take on.

4

Aaron and Trent had met the hot June day Aaron finished his long journey from Iowa. He'd gotten off the bus in White Horse just as he'd been instructed and was walking the final distance to the Eabys' farm, through the lush green farmland of late spring. The Eaby farm was another couple of miles away.

Heat shimmered off the macadam, no breeze eased the air, and beneath Aaron's backpack his shirt was damp with sweat. He squinted against the bright sun, his straw hat giving little help against the burning brilliance. He studied the well-kept farms and the neat rows of corn shoots as he passed. Everywhere he saw prosperity and order. He'd heard Lancaster County Amish were so successful in large part because of the fertile soil. He was just east of the county line, but the prosperity had obviously crossed the line too.

Cars drove past, leaving gusts of hot air in their wake. A gray-sided buggy approached. The bearded man driving it tipped his hat as he drew abreast, and Aaron nodded back. The man drove on with the clop of hooves and the rattle of wheels.

A car approached from behind and surprised Aaron by pulling to a stop beside him. He hadn't expected a ride, but when he saw the sleek black convertible with its top up, all he could think about was air-conditioning. When the driver rolled down the passenger window and said, "Hop in. It's too hot for walking," the silken voice of temptation had been too strong to resist.

He had his hand on the latch when he realized he should clarify things. "I'm going to Eabys' farm on Beaver Dam Road, which is on the other side of Route 10." He held his breath. What if it was too far out of the man's way? But air-conditioning!

"I know the road, and we can find the farm. Come on."

Aaron climbed in and sighed at the coolness. He set his backpack at his feet and laid his head against the rest.

Trent eyed the backpack. "You running away from home?"

Aaron laughed. "I've run all the way from Iowa."

Trent drove, easily taking a couple of quick turns in the road. He passed a field full of black cows with wide white stripes around their middles.

"I haven't seen cows like that before." Aaron was fascinated.

"Belties." Trent slowed as they studied them. "Formally known as Belted Galloways. They're beef cattle."

They passed a house with a beautiful garden along the road. Aaron felt a pang of homesickness as he thought how much his mother would enjoy seeing it. Her garden was a thing of beauty—half flowers, half vegetables.

"Why all the flowers?" the bishop had asked once. "They are frivolous. They do nothing. A few petunias or marigolds to keep the rabbits away, fine. But so many? Now vegetables, they are practical."

His mother smiled at her flowers. "They show me *Gott*'s glory. They remind me to praise Gott for loving us so much He gave us such beauty."

Another turn and the men passed a field of miniature horses. Aaron eyed Trent. "Are you from here? You seem to know the area well."

"I do. I grew up in Honey Brook. My family's home is a couple of miles north and I'm visiting for a couple of weeks. And I'm hungry. What about you? There's a diner near here that serves a great hamburger. Interested?"

Aaron's stomach rumbled at the thought.

Trent took that for a yes and turned north on Route 10. They sped up a large hill. Aaron grinned inside as Trent hit the brakes and slowed to a crawl behind a buggy. Trent's mechanical horsepower was brought to a near halt by one Amish horse. They inched up the hill.

"The buggies in this area are strange to my eyes," Aaron said.

"How so?" Trent asked.

"Ours are black. Yours are gray. And they're a slightly different shape."

"Farther west they're yellow or white or even a rusty orange, depending on your district."

"Yellow?" Aaron couldn't imagine it.

Cars began to line up behind Trent, but he couldn't pass because they couldn't see over the crest of the hill. And thank goodness Trent hadn't risked it. A huge semi with chain-store advertising emblazoned on its side crested the rise and sailed past them, leaving a great *whoosh* of air in its wake. A second semi appeared right behind it.

"Lots of big rigs going up and down this road, so it's almost never safe to pass here," Trent said. "The turnpike is just a few miles north." They crested the hill and saw the way was clear. Trent passed the buggy. "Lots of buggies along here too. I always get a kick out of one of the trucks crawling along behind a buggy."

They passed a large greenhouse and a small roadside store. "Run by Amish," Trent said. "My mother likes to come to the nursery for plants and the store for fresh fruit and veggies. And shoofly pies."

Another turn and the diner appeared. The two men sat across from each other on red plastic benches. Their food was served on a black Formica tabletop. Aaron decided Trent had been right. His cheeseburger was delicious.

"Tell me why you're here if you live in Iowa." Trent dipped a fry in ketchup.

Aaron explained about the Eabys' accident and their need for help with the farm, especially the horses. "I'm not sure how long I'll be here, but I see it as a chance to think without my family or everyone in our district peering over my shoulder. I want to set my own path by my decisions, not by pressure from others, no matter how well-meaning."

Trent froze with a fry halfway to his mouth and stared at Aaron. "I know just what you mean."

Aaron must have shown his skepticism without meaning to because Trent said, "I understand. I really do." He ate the fry.

"At my age most of my brothers were already married."

Trent laughed. "But you're not ready?"

"I haven't met anybody I want to marry." Besides, marrying meant he had to get baptized and join the church. And he wasn't sure that was what he wanted.

"I haven't either, and it's a good thing. I've been uncertain about career things for too long to even think about dating. It's only now that I'm stable enough to even consider dragging a woman into my life."

"You don't seem all that unstable," Aaron pointed out.

"Maybe that was the wrong word. But my father wants me to follow in his footsteps, and I don't want to. Make that I'm not *going* to."

"And you don't know how to tell him." Aaron knew that feeling well. "What does your father do?"

"He's a surgeon."

"Like cuts people open when they're sick?" Aaron was impressed. He couldn't imagine such a risky career. He also couldn't imagine going to school all those years to learn all the things that were necessary. "So you're supposed to be a surgeon too?"

"But I don't want to be. I really don't. I thought I could do it, but I realized how foolish it is to try to fit into someone else's mold."

"So if you're not a doctor, what will you be?"

"Oh, I'll be a doctor. I've graduated from medical school and done one year of residency. I want to be a doctor."

"But not a surgeon."

"No." Trent signaled the waitress for another glass of water. "Dad says I'm just burned out from all the years of study, but that's not it. I enjoy learning. I always have."

"If you don't want to be a surgeon, then what?"

"A family doctor. I like working with the variety of problems and people."

"I should think your father would be happy with you being any kind of doctor." Like his own father should be happy with him being any kind of Christian. "I know I'm not anything like a doctor, but I took an EMT course and ran with the ambulance crew back home."

"Wow, really?"

The question irritated Aaron. It was a typical *Englisher* reaction to an Amish man doing something outsiders considered unusual for his people. He sighed at the spurt of anger, chalking it up to weariness from the long journey. He knew Trent, who had been nothing but kind, meant no offense.

As if to prove it, Trent smiled. "That's certainly admirable."

"At first my father didn't like my doing it." Aaron grinned. His father's frown of disapproval had been something to behold. "He thought I would be mixing too much with the world, but when my mother burned herself and I knew what to do for her, then it was good."

"You proved yourself to him."

"Sort of. I'd prove myself more if I did something he thought worthwhile, like joining the church and marrying."

"You don't want to be Amish?"

"I don't know. I've tried English things like the EMT course and getting my driver's license, and while I like them and see their benefit,

I'm not ready to turn my back yet. I'm also not ready to join. I think my indecision is what's bothering my father."

"You're here now, away from him. You could do or be anything you want."

Aaron moved his glass, making circles in the puddle of condensation beneath it. "He wants me to be like all my brothers—I have five older brothers, all married like good Amish men. My younger brother shows every sign of being a good Amish man too. He's courting a girl and set to join the church. I'm the lone holdout."

Trent studied him. "Why would you stay Amish if you're so unsure? Maybe if you answer that question, you'll know what you should do."

Aaron gazed out the window at the cars parked in the lot. He watched a buggy move slowly down the street and a pickup swerve around it. Buggy or pickup? That was his question.

Trent studied him. "There are lots of restrictions to Amish life. I don't understand many of them, but I understand they're there to preserve faith and family."

Aaron eyed his new friend. He was an insightful man.

Trent continued, "I think you can love God and serve Him without being as strict as the Amish are. I think the rules are just that—rules. They don't necessarily make you a better person. That's a matter of the heart. My understanding is that the Amish use their rules as a way to extend their dedication to God to every aspect of their lives. But I think even they would say that it doesn't make them more Christian than others. It's just how they choose to worship."

They fell silent as the waitress cleared away their dishes. She refilled Aaron's iced tea and brought both men a slice of pie.

Trent cut a bite and hesitated before lifting it to his mouth. "If you don't remain Amish, will you be shunned? I've always thought that was a pretty heavy burden to lay on someone."

"It is, and it's supposed to be. It's to make you think about your sin, repent, and come back to the Lord and the community. I won't be shunned, because I haven't yet joined the church. But my family would never understand, and there'd be a wedge between us. If I married an Englisher . . ." He shook his head. "They'd have a hard time accepting her."

"So if you leave you're free, but you're not because you've lost so much. And if you stay, you're making people happy, but you're not free. It seems to me your real question is which way you'll feel you've lost the least."

Aaron swallowed the last bite of his blueberry pie. Whichever way he went, he feared he'd regret it forever. He looked up to find Trent watching him thoughtfully.

"I wonder," Trent said, "if there's a way we can help each other."

5

When Aubrey pulled into the lane of her grandparents' farm Monday evening after work, she kept a careful eye out for children. Since everyone in the extended family was here for her grandmother's eightieth birthday, little people were everywhere.

In the side yard, a girl of eight—if Aubrey remembered Maggie's age correctly—drove a child's wagon stuffed with little people. The miniature horse pulling them tramped patiently back and forth across the yard as the children shrieked and giggled.

Two little guys, their blond hair flying out beneath their straw hats, chased a rooster around over by the barn. The rooster ran for his life, his normal king-of-the-world strut giving way to flat-out panic.

A cluster of boys waited for their turn to swing on the tire hanging from the large maple shading the porch. They giggled and pushed and were unable to stand still, like boys the world over.

The teenage cousins were setting up a volleyball net on the far side of the barn. Lately that game had become the activity of choice at the local young people's social gatherings.

She spotted her father, a standout in his blue polo shirt, khaki pants, and shaven face, where he stood talking near the barn. Uncle James, his arms flying, must have just told the punchline of his joke because they all laughed.

She smiled at them as she climbed the stairs with her contribution to the feast in her arms, a large sheet cake reading *Happy 80th Birthday* that she'd picked up at the supermarket. Aubrey knew from experience that the food tables would be laden with several other baked goodies—brownies, pies, cookies, fruit crumbles—but she carried the official cake, the one the candles would be put on.

She made her way into the house, which was crammed with women and food. Many called a greeting, and she found her mother standing at the sink, washing various utensils as they were dirtied. Aunt Edna stood beside her and dried—and talked. Mom said Aunt Edna's spiritual gift was gab. Here in this room all the conversation swirled in Dutch.

Aubrey caught her mother's eye and winked. Mom grinned. In between gossip about people Mom didn't know, Aunt Edna always said the same things: "How could you leave us? You've broken our mother's heart. Come back!" And Mom always smiled and said nothing. Aunt Edna would never understand.

Aubrey had barely set the cake in the space saved for it on the dessert table when a baby was thrust at her.

"Here. Hold Tabitha." Aubrey's cousin Rachel let go before Aubrey had her arms around the child, so Aubrey had to scramble to keep Tabitha from ending up in a heap on the floor. The baby was bald with huge brown eyes and a somewhat unnerving stare.

"How are you?" Aubrey asked the baby, feeling as if she should say something to her. After all, other women talked nonstop to infants.

No answer. No smile. Just the stare.

Aubrey tried again. "How old are you?"

"She's seven months," called Rachel. "She can't talk yet."

"I knew that," Aubrey told Rachel, who didn't seem convinced.

Aubrey trailed Rachel, who knelt before an unhappy toddler sitting with two little cousins about her age in a corner where they wouldn't get in the way of the work being done around them. The other two children had a toy in each hand. Rachel's little one had none and wore a woebegone expression.

Rachel leaned in, kissed one of the other children, and gently took one of the wooden blocks. She handed it to her tyke, whose face cleared immediately. She leaned in and again kissed the child she'd appropriated the toy from. Aubrey couldn't hear what she said, but the kid beamed.

Amazing.

Aubrey gave a little squeak as Tabitha grabbed her hoop earring and tugged. "No no, sweetie." She pulled the pudgy hand away. The baby continued to stare.

As always unsure what to do in the whirlwind of meal preparations, Aubrey stood to the side, bouncing Tabitha. She marveled at the affinity these women had for kitchens and kitchen work. She never knew what to do in that room unless expressly told, especially when it was someone else's kitchen. She could do all sorts of things like help a patient regain use of his legs after a bad accident or reach for the ceiling after rotator cuff surgery, but somehow the magical ability to automatically know what to do in a kitchen had passed her by.

What if she'd been raised Amish and hadn't liked kitchens? Or housework? Or needlework? Talk about a round hole and a square peg. She couldn't imagine herself making a shoofly pie, let alone a quilt. She was a woman who loved restaurants and online shopping.

In the clear division of responsibilities that marked most Amish families, the women were keepers of the home. Not that they didn't do other chores as needed. She'd seen many an Amish wife working in the fields at planting and harvesting, driving teams of six horses with ease, but home was where these women flourished—and were expected to flourish.

She watched her aunts and adult cousins set out the array of food. Her mother stood out in a knit shirt in shades of green and blue with a pair of navy slacks, but she managed to work easily with the other women in their dresses, aprons, and Kapps. Her ease came from having been raised in this milieu until she was eighteen.

The baby grabbed a fistful of Aubrey's hair and pulled. Aubrey's chin-length bob, swinging free instead of caught back, was too fascinating for the baby to resist.

"Easy, sweetie." She worked the little hand free and kissed the palm. She blew a raspberry on the soft skin. Tabitha was unimpressed. "You want your mommy?" The baby blinked.

Aubrey cast about for Rachel, but she had gone onto the porch to check on her two other children. Aubrey could hear her call their names.

Rachel had four children: Tabitha, the little one in the corner now sharing toys, and the two outside. And Rachel was a year younger than Aubrey's twenty-seven. Aubrey took a deep breath. Her cousins were all married with multiple children except for Bess, who was the schoolteacher at the small white building down the road, and Aubrey herself.

"Come November Louisa's getting married," Rachel said as she breezed up to check on Tabitha. She indicated one of the younger cousins.

"Isn't she ten years old?" Aubrey asked.

"It does seem that way, doesn't it?" Rachel smiled. "She's eighteen. Are you and Tabitha okay? I'd like to help with getting the drinks ready."

Aubrey looked at the baby, who stared back. "We're fine."

And Rachel was gone.

Aubrey's arms were beginning to tire. For a little thing, Tabitha was surprisingly heavy. Aubrey saw her grandmother sitting in her favorite rocker. She was wearing her starched white organdy apron for the occasion, probably last worn on her wedding day and put away for her funeral. It tickled Aubrey that *Mammi* would break tradition and get away with it. She'd been a widow for fifteen years now and lived in the annex, or *Daadi Haus*. Her oldest son lived in the main house and worked the farm.

"Mammi! Happy Birthday!" Aubrey leaned in to kiss her grandmother's wrinkled cheek.

"*Mein* Aubrey." Mammi smiled and patted her hand. She frowned at Tabitha and whispered, "Whose *Bobbeli* is this?" She glanced around to be certain no one was listening. "I must confess that I can't always keep them straight."

"How many grands and great-grands do you have?"

Mammi smiled with pride. "Thirty-five grandchildren and forty-five great-grandchildren and counting."

Aubrey thought of her family with just her and her brother. Neither was married. When they were, they probably wouldn't help swell the count very much. Fortunately, Mammi was able to have the large family she loved without their help, and Aubrey was glad for that.

She set the baby in Mammi's lap. "This is Rachel's and her name's Tabitha." Tabitha transferred her stare to her great-grandmother.

Mammi ran a finger down the baby's cheek and murmured sweet nothings in a soft flow of Pennsylvania Dutch. Tabitha smiled, her eyes crinkling to slits.

Aubrey had to remember that trick for next time she held a baby, though she wasn't sure what had secured Tabitha's happiness: the finger on the cheek or the soft flow of words. Or maybe it was just Mammi.

Someone tapped on her shoulder.

"Come talk to me," hissed a dramatic voice in her ear. "*Please* come talk to me."

Bekka. When the girl had been eight and announced she was no longer Rebecca but Bekka with two *k*'s, it should have been a warning.

Aubrey followed her seventeen-year-old cousin onto the porch. For the moment it was empty of children.

Bekka began pacing. "I can't stand it. I can't. All those babies!"

Who didn't like babies? Even people like Aubrey who weren't

comfortable around them didn't dislike them. But Aubrey knew babies weren't really the issue.

Bekka waved her hand. "Don't give me that look. I like babies. I just don't want to have any."

"Ever?"

She shrugged. "Maybe when I'm old like you. But all around me people are getting married like it's going out of style. My sister Louisa's wedding's in November, and she's only a year older than me." She came to a stop in front of Aubrey. "I don't want to get married. I haven't lived yet!"

"So don't get married."

"You don't know what it's like!"

Aubrey studied Bekka. "Are your parents pressuring you?"

"They keep hosting sings, and they've invited the youth for a picnic next Sunday evening. Mamm is constantly telling me about all the available guys as if I'll fall in love because of her descriptions. Just because that stuff worked for Louisa doesn't mean it'll work for me."

"Can't you just go to the picnic on Sunday and have fun? Forget the pressure? No one's going to make you marry."

Bekka's eyes were full of despair. "Two guys are trying to court me. I don't want to be courted!"

Aubrey understood the boys being attracted to Bekka. She was a very pretty young woman. Her auburn hair was thick, her cheeks naturally rosy, her lips full and pink. When Bekka laughed, she had a glow about her, some inexplainable something that radiated. Aubrey had to wonder if either of the boys interested in Bekka saw beyond the beauty to the complicated young woman inside.

"If you don't want a boyfriend or marriage, what do you want, Bekka?"

She closed her eyes. "I don't know. But I do know I want the time and freedom to figure it out. I don't want to be baptized and take my vows. I don't want to join the church yet. What if when I finally figure it all out, I don't want to be Amish? I don't want to be shunned! I love my family."

"Of course you do." Aubrey grabbed Bekka's hand and squeezed to offer what little comfort she could. She wanted to say, "There now. Relax. It'll be all right," but she bit the words back. It might not be all right. For searchers like Bekka, life could be hard, questions overwhelming, and answers an unsatisfactory gray.

Rumspringa might not be an answer for Bekka either. The outward signs of her mild rebellion were skirts hiked to her knees, a slash of bright red lipstick, and the latest cell phone. That seemed to be as wild as she wanted to be. It was clearly inside that she struggled.

The screen door opened and Rachel stepped out. She eyed Aubrey and Bekka, suspicion clear on her face. Bekka saw the expression, pulled her hand free of Aubrey's, and turned her back. "Later," she muttered to Aubrey and jumped down the stairs. She disappeared around the side of the house.

"Don't infect her." Rachel's tone was cold.

Aubrey took a deep breath at the unfounded accusation. She forced herself to speak evenly. "She doesn't need me to give her ideas, Rachel. She has a mind of her own."

Rachel sniffed, then rang the bell hanging beside the door. "Dinner!" she called to the men and children, who came eagerly. Before she went back inside, she threw one last glance at Aubrey. "Don't."

6

When Trent had met Aaron by sheer chance, he had been driving aimlessly in the Mercedes convertible his parents had given him for medical school graduation. Even as he thanked them, he'd thought how impractical the car was. And pretentious for someone his age. He was still a student and would be for several more years.

But the car was undoubtedly a joy to drive, and so he had been killing time until he could return to the five-acre gentleman's farm his parents owned just north of Honey Brook. He'd slid to a stop beside the Amish man and offered him a ride.

Not that he believed the Amish guy was about to have heatstroke. He was undoubtedly a lot tougher physically than Trent with all the physical labor the Amish embraced. Trent just wanted his mind occupied with something besides his own jumbled thoughts. Talking to someone might help disperse what plagued him.

He glanced at his watch. His mom, dad, and twin sisters should be halfway to the airport by now. He felt his shoulders relax. He wouldn't have to face his father again today.

This morning he and Dad had yelled at each other, actually raised their voices. Usually Dad stated his opinion—which he expected Trent to take as seriously as Moses took the Ten Commandments from God—and Trent did nothing but fume inside at the heavy-handed treatment.

But this morning? As he thought back on his defiant attitude, he flushed. He might as well be thirteen again for all the finesse he'd shown. The whole conversation had been conducted in exclamation points.

"It's my choice, Dad!"

"Not if I'm paying the bills!"

"Then don't pay my bills!"

"I've paid your way your whole life!"

"I thought that's what parents did for their kids if they could!"

"You change specialties and you'll be on your own! Not a dime from me!"

"I'm changing whether you support me or not!"

When he stalked from Dad's study before he said something he'd really regret, his jaw was set and his fists were clenched. Half an hour later when he kissed his mother and the girls goodbye, he was still breathing heavily.

As he gave his mother a bear hug, she hugged him back. "It'll work out," she whispered in his ear. "You do what you must. He'll come around."

Whether Dad would come around or not, the decision was Trent's to make, and he'd made it. He'd already done the paperwork and the interview. All that remained was the final approval.

He studied the suitcases and backpacks waiting in the front hall. Dad was actually leaving for vacation, an amazing thing for such a control freak. This trip was the last hoorah before the girls began their summer jobs, then left for college. Dad did love his girls.

Well, so did Trent. They were ten years younger than he, coming along when football and baseball had been the most important things in his young life. Dad had taken him to the hospital to meet them the morning after their midnight arrival. When he'd sat in the ugly vinyl chair in his mother's room and they'd placed a baby in the crook of each arm, he'd fallen in love.

It hadn't made sense. They were red and bald and helpless, anything but beautiful. Still, every protective gene he'd possessed stood at attention, and he became their superhero. He'd made it his duty to watch over them until he left for college when they were eight and full of sass.

Even thinking about them now made him smile. They'd been the cutest little girls and had grown into beautiful young women. They had Dad's backbone tempered by Mom's grace and kindness. He hoped his facing down Dad would make things easier for them if they had to make independent decisions their father disagreed with.

"Have a wonderful time on vacation." He'd hugged each girl, lifting her off her feet so she squealed.

"We will." Olivia's excitement was palpable as she danced around the room.

"I wish you were coming with us." Victoria hugged him extra tight, her tender heart making her teary-eyed over a big brother staying home.

"You'll do fine without me." So would Dad. "All those mountains and valleys and beautiful sights will impress you so much you'll forget I'm not there."

"We won't forget. Who could forget you?" Olivia grinned at him.

His mother took his hand between hers and squeezed. She glanced toward the study where Dad could be heard moving around. "He loves you, you know."

Trent sighed. "I know. And I love him." He kissed her cheek. "But I have to say you are a saint to put up with him."

She shrugged. "He doesn't want *me* to join his practice."

"And that's a good thing," Olivia said. "You're an equestrienne, not a doctor."

"As are you." Mom smiled at the girls but kept her grip on Trent's hand. "Prizewinning equestriennes no less."

"Which is why we're going riding in Wyoming!" Olivia continued to bounce.

Victoria picked up her backpack with a sigh. "It'll be one of those things where you walk behind a leader, and we'll be bored silly. Just watch."

Mom went up on tiptoe and kissed Trent. "Don't forget—"

"I know. The horses. I won't." Three much-loved mares lived in the barn out back.

He heard footsteps from the direction of the study. He gave each of the girls and his mother another quick hug and left. He would not send them all off with the sharp words lurking on his tongue, words that would certainly erupt if he saw his father again.

So he drove and drove, muttering under his breath for the first half hour. By the time he found Aaron, he'd regained most of his emotional equilibrium. As he ate his lunch and talked with the Amish man, he was amazed at the similarities in their circumstances. Who would have thought?

After he left Aaron at the Eaby farm, Trent went home to an empty house. The silence was wonderful. Usually life was so full of people that he yearned for a quiet place he could escape to. Now he had quiet for two full weeks!

He dropped into the recliner in the family room and turned on the television just because he could. He never had free time during the day—or the evening for that matter. He flipped channels until he stumbled on an old Clint Eastwood spaghetti western. An hour and a half later he turned the set off and leaned his head back. He was going to take a nap—again, just because he could.

So he passed the next few days. It was, after all, his vacation. He swam each day, lounging by the pool and enjoying every lazy minute.

He went to the diner for dinner Friday and Saturday nights and ordered in pizza on Sunday. He watched lots of TV, amazed at some of the strange reality shows considered worthy of attention.

The one chore he did conscientiously was care for the horses. The three of them lived in equine luxury in a stone barn that, with only a few modifications, would have made a wonderful home for a human family of five. Each morning he led them from their stalls to pasture, and each evening he brought them back, brushing, watering, and feeding them. They were well-behaved animals, making the task both relaxing and pleasant.

On Monday, Trent rose from watching television and knew he had to get out or go nuts. A man could only take so much relaxation. He'd go check on Aaron and see how he was doing at the Eabys'. He promised himself a short visit so he wouldn't get in Aaron's way. Maybe he'd ask if Aaron wanted to go to the diner again.

He enjoyed his visit so much on Monday that he decided to go back on Tuesday. When Trent drove down the short lane to the Eabys' place, he was impressed anew with the many indications of hard work. The vegetable patch was weeded and the grass was neatly trimmed. The little shed held fresh asparagus, lettuce, and luscious-looking strawberries, as well as jams and jellies. The prosperous appearance was amazing considering the accident that had sidelined Mahlon and Miriam. The only thing that made him wonder was the barbecue sign for Friday night.

As he climbed from the convertible, a young woman walked onto the porch and called, "Asa!" A boy of about ten came running from the field where he'd been picking strawberries. He grinned as he ran to the young woman, and she beamed back at him.

Trent's breath caught in his throat. What a lovely smile—warm, spontaneous, and without guile. It made her eyes crinkle almost shut. He'd never before realized how attractive that scrunch could be on someone.

He had no idea what she said to the boy, but he scurried off to do her bidding. She glanced at Trent, and he stared at her. *Smile, you dolt!* But she turned away and went inside before the message made it from his brain to his lips. Which was good. She was obviously Amish with that dress and the Kapp with the little puffs that gave it its trademark heart shape. And an Amish woman was not for him.

Aaron walked from the barn, hand raised in greeting. After a few minutes of chitchat, Trent cleared his throat.

"The young woman who came onto the porch—that wasn't Miriam Eaby, was it?" A *married* Amish woman was even further off-limits.

Aaron raised his eyebrows and cocked his head, making commentary without saying a word. Trent tried not to color, but he felt heat suffuse his face.

"Did she have scrapes and bruises on her face, her arm in a cast, and probably a small child hanging from her skirts?"

Trent pushed aside the relief he felt. "No, no bruises or scrapes. No cast. No kid."

"Then it wasn't Miriam. It was Sally. She's here to help out."

Sally. She was single. He was sure of that. She wouldn't be here otherwise. She'd be at home caring for her own family.

He swallowed his smile. What did it matter? She was Amish, he reminded himself. Unavailable to him. Still he asked, "Is she local or did she come from a distance?" He tried to keep his tone casual, as if he were just making small talk.

"She's local, I hear. Interested?" Aaron's mischievous grin said he saw right through Trent's seemingly innocent question.

Trent held up a hand. He needed to change the subject fast. "So tell me about the horses. Is Peaceable any better today?"

Aaron led Trent to the pasture where they watched Peaceable ignore the world and discussed him at length. Trent had no wisdom to impart. "Sometimes nasty is just nasty and will never change. What does Mahlon say?"

"Keep trying, but I don't know if it'll do any good. If the animal doesn't want to cooperate, we can't make him."

"He's like some people who make their lives more difficult by their attitudes."

"'A merry heart does good like medicine,'" Aaron quoted.

"Exactly!" Trent thought of the crinkly-eyed smile. She would do him good. Somehow he just knew it. If only she wasn't Amish.

"Want to go to the diner for dinner?"

"If I can find Jake and let him know I'll be gone."

They walked through the barn, then checked the shed. No Jake.

"He's probably sleeping under a tree somewhere. Maybe over by the creek." Aaron indicated the swift flow of water across the street.

A blue car turned into the lane, and Trent noticed Aaron perk up at the sight. Not that Aaron had been sloughing off, but he was more alert, more alive somehow. The car parked, and a very attractive young woman climbed out.

She caught sight of Aaron and waved. Aaron hurried to greet her, and it was Trent's turn to smirk at a friend's reaction to a pretty face as he followed.

"I came to get some strawberries," the woman was saying when Trent joined her and Aaron. "My mother will love them for dessert."

"My favorite way to eat them is to dunk them in confectioner's sugar," Aaron said as he walked her to the shed.

"Sounds delicious." She stepped into the shade of the little building. The boy, who had gone back to picking strawberries, came running again. Trent looked to the porch, hoping the girl with the wonderful smile would come out again to check on the boy, but no such luck.

"Trent, this is Aubrey," Aaron said.

She held out her hand. "Aubrey Green."

Trent shook it. "Pleased to meet you."

"Aubrey's the physical therapist who's treating Mahlon and Miriam." Aubrey picked up two containers of strawberries and a head of lettuce. The boy went behind the little counter and worked a small calculator. Aubrey handed him her money, and he counted out her change.

"These look delicious," she said, popping a berry into her mouth and discarding the stem. "Nice meeting you, Trent." She turned to Aaron and her gaze lingered on him a moment before she said, "Goodbye, Aaron." With a wave, she climbed back into her car.

Aaron stood and watched as she drove away.

"She's English," Trent said.

Aaron thumbed his suspenders. "I noticed."

7

On Wednesday Aubrey drove toward the Eabys' place, telling herself her eagerness was because she was looking forward to working with Mahlon and Miriam. She was going to encourage them. She was going to help them heal more quickly. She was—

She sighed. While that was certainly true, a small voice inside asked, "Do you really expect me to believe that?" It was bad enough she'd come back to buy strawberries and lettuce yesterday when neither she nor her mother needed any. But it had worked.

She bit back a grin. Maybe she'd see him again today. She rolled her eyes at herself. She was as bad as a teenager hoping for a glimpse of her latest crush.

As she crested a hill on the winding road, she noticed a horse and sulky in a field bordering the road. The field was full of weeds and cutoff cornstalks from last year's harvest. As she watched, she realized she'd never seen a buggy horse in a field before. The big draft horses worked the fields in teams, pulling plows and various pieces of farming equipment. Buggy horses, smaller and more delicately built, were for the roads.

The sulky driver, a young man in Amish clothing, clearly wanted the horse to go through the field and was swinging his whip to emphasize his wishes. Aubrey frowned. How could a buggy horse pull a narrow-wheeled conveyance like a sulky through dirt? Wouldn't the wheels sink into the soil and the weeds clog the spokes? It took teams of the huge horses to pull wagons through the fields.

Aubrey's breath caught. The driver wasn't merely swinging his whip to urge the horse on. He was bringing it down again and again on the horse's back.

The horse, upset at the pain of the slashing whip and unhappy at the strange things underfoot as they lashed against his legs, twisted and reared in the traces as he fought to get free. Of course he couldn't, held in place as he was by bridle, reins, and shafts.

She wanted to scream at the driver to stop, but he just intensified his brutal treatment. Aubrey found herself flinching with each crack of the whip.

The driver of the sulky must have seen her out of the corner of his eye and noted her slowing down and her horrified expression. He faced her and lowered the hand with the whip.

A car came over the hill behind her, forcing her to drive on. She glanced back, and the sulky driver was watching her car. She knew that as soon as she was out of sight, he'd use that whip again.

But what could she do? It wasn't her horse. It wasn't her field. She didn't know the story of how they got where they were. Was it actually abuse, or was the driver just a strong disciplinarian? She replayed what she had seen. No, it was abuse. She was sure of it. But if she called the authorities, the man could be gone by the time anyone got there. She couldn't describe him beyond his being Amish, and there were hundreds of Amish men in the area and hundreds of chestnut horses. The sulky wasn't a typical sight. That could be a clue. Just so no one thought it was Aaron because of the sulky.

Aaron. She needed to talk to him. Since he drove a sulky for training purposes, maybe he knew others who did too. He'd know what to do.

She pulled into the Eabys' lane. "Aaron?" she called as she climbed from the car. "Aaron!"

No one came. She ran to the barn and called again. No answer.

She ran to the pastures. Nothing there but the grazing horses, who raised their heads curiously when she appeared. What should she do?

Mahlon should know what to do. He might even know who the man was.

She grabbed her bag of supplies and hurried toward the house. Mahlon opened the front door just as she raised her hand to knock. Several children surrounded him, eagerly pressing forward. Even baby Naomi was part of the welcoming committee, held in her big sister Anna's arms.

She made herself smile and be calm as she stepped inside. She didn't want to upset the little ones. "Be careful not to bump your father. We don't want him to fall down, do we?"

The five children all smiled at her in spite of the fact that they didn't understand her English. Sally and Miriam were in the kitchen starting preparations for the evening meal, and Miriam repeated Aubrey's warning in Dutch. All the children nodded solemnly. In spite of her agitation, Aubrey had to grin at their serious expressions. The little girls had their hair pulled back and knotted at the base of their necks but wore no Kapps. The little boys had bangs and Dutch-boy bobs. They were so cute.

She turned to Mahlon and quietly asked, "What do I do if I saw someone mistreating his horse?"

Mahlon's brow furrowed. "Mistreating how?"

"Using a whip. Making him pull a sulky through a field."

"A sulky?" Mahlon took a deep breath. "I'll take care of it."

Aubrey blinked. Relief washed through her. "Do you know who it was?"

He held up a hand. "I'll take care of it."

And she realized the conversation was finished, the topic closed. Was it the community taking care of one of its own? Was it because an outsider dared to interfere?

She swallowed and forced herself to switch gears. It was time to do her job. She watched Mahlon maneuver about the room on his crutches. "You're doing well," she told him, pleased. His upper body, strong from all the work on the farm and with the horses, handled the weight of his lower body with ease.

"It's not so bad once I get downstairs," he said. "My biggest challenge is not bumping into—" He indicated the five little ones who moved and bobbed, coming together and separating in ever-changing patterns like bits of glass in a kaleidoscope.

Aubrey glanced at the ceiling, toward the bedrooms on the upper floor. "How do you manage on the stairs?"

"It's hard. I can go up easily enough, but coming down? I sit and lower myself step by step." He laughed, and the children joined him, though they had no idea what was funny.

Aubrey had to smile at the image too. She reached into her bag and pulled out a set of ten-pound barbells. "I know zipping around on the crutches helps keep your upper body strong, but using these weights will help too. Sit in one of the kitchen chairs without arms, and we'll go through the series of exercises I'd like you to do every day."

Mahlon sat. She handed him the weights and pulled out a set of five-pounders for herself. "Arms at your sides. Lift the weights in a bicep curl." She demonstrated.

Ten minutes and several other patterns later, Aubrey smiled. She reached back into her bag and pulled out a sheet. "Here are the instructions in writing with illustrations."

Mahlon took the sheet and studied it. "*Denke.*"

"I have something else for you." She reached in her bag and pulled out a flat plastic disc filled with air that allowed the disc to undulate. She held it out to Mahlon.

"For me?" Mahlon stared at the disc. "What do I do with it?"

"You sit on it."

Mahlon eyed the disc suspiciously.

"While you're limited in your movement because you can't put any weight on your bad leg, you want some way to keep your body strong. That will make the rehab much easier when the bones have healed. One way to keep your core active is to sit on the balance disc and let your muscles react as it moves under you."

She put the disc on a chair and moved in a small circle to demonstrate. "Try it." She stood and indicated the chair.

He sat, cast-covered leg held straight out. For a few seconds he sat rigid, then slowly relaxed. "What do I do now?"

"Just sit. You can do Miriam's exercises with her and the *Kinder*." Only as she said *Kinder* did Aubrey realize they were speaking Dutch. She darted a glance at Miriam, remembering her request to speak English around the children. Had she offended her? Miriam just shrugged, and Aubrey relaxed, continuing in that language, leading Miriam in her hand exercises. Mahlon and the children did the movements too. Once or twice, Mahlon overbalanced on the disc and his arms windmilled as he tried to right himself, his eyes comically wide. When he realized that this amused his children, he faked it several more times.

When they were finished, the house was redolent with the wonderful fragrances of the dinner Sally was preparing. Aubrey gathered her supplies, leaving the weights and disc for Mahlon.

"I'll be back in two days. Do your exercises."

As she crossed the porch, she looked again toward the barn. As before, no one with a charming smile appeared. She was amazed at how disappointed she felt. *For heaven's sake*, she upbraided herself. She'd only met the guy two days ago. Could she be any more foolish? *Remember Ethan. Remember your bank account. And remember Aaron's Amish.*

Yeah, but that smile. She realized *she* was smiling at the thought of it.

"What's so funny?" Asa and Ben appeared beside her as if by magic, shirttails hanging out, hats pushed back, and the scent of freshly picked strawberries wafting in their wake.

"Nothing's funny." She certainly wasn't telling them it was Aaron's smile, and anyway it wasn't so much funny as sweet.

"Then why are you smiling?" They followed her to the car. Once there they forgot the smile as they stared at her car.

"It's square," Asa said, clearly puzzled.

"It gives me lots of space in the back to carry my equipment."

They ran hands over the smooth metal, warm to their touch in the sunshine.

Asa glanced at the house, then at Aubrey. "Can I sit in it?"

"Me too?" Ben said. "After him. Behind the wheel."

Aubrey blinked. "I-I don't know."

"We won't hurt anything," Asa assured her.

"I never thought you would. It's just that I don't want you to get in trouble. You know."

The boys did know. She was certain they had ridden in cars. Amish taxis were a big thing in the area. Vans were hired to take whole families to doctors, to chiropractors, to visit friends who lived at a distance, or to go to one of the large markets. Retired English men and women could make a nice side income as Amish drivers.

But she was sure it wasn't riding in the car that intrigued the boys. It was *driving* it. They wanted to sit behind the wheel and imagine themselves pushing the pedal to the floor as they sped down the highway, the wind blowing through their hair and the miles disappearing behind them.

How convenient it would be if Mahlon came outside right now and gave her some silent indication of whether he minded his boys pretending to drive. But he didn't appear. Instead, three-year-old Harper pushed the screen door open and toddled onto the porch.

"Asa! Ben!" she cried, delighted to see her big brothers.

"Get back inside, Harper," Ben called, not really paying attention to her as he inspected Aubrey's car.

"Where's Mamm? Or Sally?" Asa called.

Harper pointed back in the house.

"Go find them," he ordered. "You shouldn't be out here alone."

Harper grinned and took a step forward.

Aubrey smiled at the little cutie. "Asa's right, little one. Go find your mama." When Harper didn't move, Aubrey took a step in her direction. Asa and Ben jumped in front of her.

"Can we, Aubrey?" Asa begged. "See? We're not even dirty." He stuck his arms out so she could inspect him.

Ben followed suit. "We cleaned up so we wouldn't hurt the car."

Aubrey swallowed a grin. Apparently age or gender or both made *cleaned up* a phrase of differing definitions. She felt caught. She didn't care in the least if the boys sat in her car, but in her mind she saw her cousin Rachel at Mammi's party, scowling, saying, "Don't."

Over the boys' heads she saw Harper wave her pudgy little hand at her, then do her version of the thumb and finger touch. "Give me a minute," she told the boys. "Your sister needs help."

"*Daed*!" Asa yelled. "Harper!"

Little boys—the same everywhere.

Harper grinned as Asa shouted her name. She walked to the edge of the porch. "I come."

"No!" Aubrey shouted, but faster than she could react, the little girl stepped off the porch. An uncertain expression crossed the child's face when she realized the step was much higher than her small legs could manage. Her foot caught in her skirt. Her arms flailed. She gave a little squeak.

The little girl tumbled head over heels.

8

Aubrey was already running toward Harper as the child tumbled down the steps, her skirts flying, her hair coming unbound. She landed in a sprawl, facedown on the concrete walk.

"Harper!" Aubrey fell to her knees beside the girl, terrified of serious injury. Why hadn't she realized what the child intended? She should have. She should have prevented this. What if she'd broken a bone or damaged something vital? What if she had a bad concussion?

Then Harper rolled over and howled, going from limp rag to outraged victim in a moment. Whatever the child had injured, it wasn't her vocal cords.

When Harper tried to sit up, Aubrey put her hands gently on her shoulders. "Lie still, sweetheart. Rest a moment."

Sally and Miriam burst from the house. Mahlon hobbled out behind them.

Already a huge goose egg had risen on Harper's little forehead. Her palms were scraped and her dress had a tear at the knee, making Aubrey imagine scrapes there too. There would probably be bruises from the edges of the stair treads. But the big worry, thanks to the goose egg, was possible concussion.

Miriam fell to her knees beside her daughter. "I'm here, Harper. I'm here, mein Bobbeli. You'll be okay."

Harper let it be known she disagreed.

"Let me see. Move, boys. Let me see." The authoritative voice made

Asa and Ben step aside. Aaron lowered himself beside Harper. "Let me check her, Miriam."

Miriam stared at him, eyes wide with surprise.

"I know what I'm doing," he said, his voice calm and reassuring.

After a moment's hesitation, she nodded.

With sure and gentle hands, he checked Harper, assessing her pupils, searching for broken bones, palpating her stomach, and running his hands over her head to be certain there were no other bumps hidden in her hair. The whole time he spoke to her, words soft and indistinct but clearly comforting to the child, even if they were in a language foreign to her. Aubrey watched him with interest. He did know what he was doing.

He patted Harper on the hand, then stood. When the child tried to sit up again, he helped her. She held her arms out to Miriam, who pulled her close.

"Is she okay?" Aubrey asked. "Should we take her to the ER?" And it would be "we." The family—at least Mahlon, Miriam, and Harper—would climb into her car and she'd drive them.

Aaron smiled. "She's okay. A cold pack on the swelling and disinfectant on the scrapes will be all she needs." He glanced at Mahlon. "She'll have bruises and be sore for a few days. You should give her a painkiller every four hours as she needs it. Keep an eye on her. If she goes limp or won't stay awake, let me know."

"All right. Denke." Mahlon herded his family including Asa and Ben inside. Miriam held Harper close in her one good arm.

Aubrey eyed Aaron. "You've had medical training."

He shrugged. "I've taken enough emergency medical classes to assess Harper."

"You're a handy man to have around."

"Thanks." He smiled at her, and her heart sped up again just when it had slowed from the Harper incident.

Calm down. It was only a smile. Not knowing what else to do, she started toward her car. "Well, I guess I'll see you in a couple of days."

"Wait a minute, Audrey."

"Aubrey," she said automatically even as her heart stood on tiptoe waiting to hear what he had to say. "With a *b*."

He grinned, and she knew he knew, and had known from the first time she said her name. "You're terrible."

"I am."

And they stood grinning while the air seemed to crackle around them.

Into that expectant moment drove a sulky, rattling up the lane. She automatically turned at the noise and stared in disbelief. She'd forgotten all about the guy with the whip in the excitement over Harper. As he careened up the lane, all her anger came rushing back.

The sulky came to a halt by the barn door, and the driver jumped down as if he hadn't a care in the world. She hesitated. Was she wrong? He seemed so relaxed and casual, not like some creep who abused animals.

He turned and saw Aubrey and her car. His step hitched an instant, then kept firm as he walked to the horse's head.

That little hitch confirmed what Aubrey had realized the minute she saw him. It was the same guy. She turned to tell Aaron what she'd seen, but he was already surging forward, jaw clenched, eyes hot. "Jake! You'd better have a good explanation for this."

This meant the horse, sweating, stomping in place, wide-eyed with distress.

"It's Peaceable. You know how he is." Jake waved his hand, his manner saying clearly that the horse had created his own problems.

Aaron reached to touch the horse, but he flinched away. "And these welts?"

Jake shrugged. "He ran into a tree branch hanging over the road. Wouldn't let me steer around it. He's one headstrong boy."

"Not so." Aubrey glared at Jake.

Aaron seemed not to hear her comment as he walked slowly around the horse, examining the animal inch by inch. He glared at Jake. "There are several welts. No tree branch made these marks."

"It was a whip!" Aubrey practically shouted.

Aaron heard her this time. He stalked to the sulky, searched, and pulled out a whip. "I told you no more!"

Jake shook his head, scorn dripping from his manner. "Like you can give me orders."

Aaron just stared, expression hard and unforgiving.

Jake tried cajoling. "Come on, Aaron. It's just a horse."

"Yes, and he deserves to be treated with respect."

"Respect?" Jake gave a short bark of laughter and turned to walk away. "It's a horse, a nasty horse at that. I save my respect for where it counts, like for the bishop."

Aubrey had to wonder if even that was true.

"Don't you walk out on Peaceable." Aaron was rigid with fury. Aubrey was surprised she didn't see steam coming from his ears.

All insolence, Jake sneered over his shoulder. "I thought since you were so upset, you would take care of him."

"Who is this guy?" Aubrey held her arms at her sides to try to stop them from shaking. "What's he doing with Peaceable?"

"His name's Jake Stoltzfus and he works here."

"Mahlon employs someone who handles his horses like this?"

Aaron shrugged. "I don't get it either."

Aubrey glared at Jake's back. "When I'm finished talking to Mahlon and telling him what I saw, he won't be here anymore." Aubrey didn't know if that was true or not, but she'd sure do her best.

Jake pivoted and smirked at her. "Good luck, lady. Why should he listen to you?"

"Oh, he'll listen all right. He already has." She turned to Aaron. "This man was trying to make Peaceable pull the sulky through a field, and he was whipping him to make him do it."

Aaron frowned. "Why did you take him off the road, Jake? We're training him for traffic, not cross-country."

Aubrey didn't think she'd ever felt so angry, even when she'd been furious at Ethan. Then her anger had always been tempered by sorrow. Today she felt pure molten fury. If ever there was a time for righteous anger, it was now. "The field he was trying to force Peaceable through was full of knee-high weeds and chopped-off cornstalks that kept hitting the horse's legs."

Aaron bent to inspect Peaceable's legs. When he straightened, he indicated the road with an outstretched arm, index finger pointing. "Get out. Take your things and go."

Jake curled his lip. "You can't fire me. You're just some cousin from Iowa who can't even speak correctly. If anybody goes, you do."

Aubrey turned to find Mahlon on the porch, watching, listening. How long had he been there?

"Bring the horse here, Aaron," Mahlon called.

Aaron released the animal from the traces and took him by the bridle. "Come on, boy. It's okay now. Shh. We're going to take good care of you." The horse went reluctantly.

Mahlon awkwardly used his crutches to come down the steps. He studied the horse, walking slowly around the sweating and trembling beast. When he finished, he turned a calm face to Jake. Sometimes anger was red-hot, but sometimes it was all ice. Mahlon's gaze could have caused frostbite at the equator. Jake actually shivered.

Mahlon rested a hand against Peaceable's neck. "I have a lot of money invested in this horse, Jake. I need to turn him around as quickly as I can. I'm already behind schedule because of the accident. Now because of Peaceable's injuries and the emotional trauma you've caused, I will be further behind." He spoke each word calmly and precisely. It was worse than if he'd roared at the other man. "I will not allow you to damage my reputation as a trainer by your strange need to prove—I don't even know what."

Jake stretched his hand toward Peaceable. "He's all right, Mahlon. I didn't hurt him." Peaceable jerked away from his touch. "He's—he's all right," Jake repeated as if saying it would make it so.

Mahlon didn't respond to the foolish comment. "I hired you at the bishop's request. 'He needs someone to take him under his wing, someone to show him how things should be done,' the bishop said. I confess I didn't want to take you on, Jake. I know your father and mother. They are fine people. I know your brothers. They are fine men. I also know your reputation."

Aubrey watched Mahlon with interest. The quiet Amish man had a steely backbone.

"But the bishop wanted me to help you, and Miriam agreed. The bishop is my leader, and I felt I should do as he requested."

Mahlon took a deep breath. At this point Aubrey saw the ice of anger tempered by sorrow. "I know I will disappoint the bishop and those hoping for your salvation, Jake, and I'm sorry for that. I know I will disappoint my wife. But I cannot jeopardize my reputation, my family, or my animals." The ice returned. "What if you had driven this distressed horse into the yard when Harper fell?"

"What fall? When?" Jake demanded.

Mahlon ignored the questions. "I will forgive you for trying to take advantage of me and my kindness, but I will not allow you to continue in this behavior. I would be doing all of us a great disservice if I did. I will just say to you what Jesus said: 'Go and sin no more.'"

"But you need me!" Jake's arrogance was gone, and Aubrey saw fear.

Mahlon suddenly seemed weary and weighed down. "Aaron, will you take care of Peaceable, please? I'd do it myself, but I think you're going to need two good legs to handle such an unhappy animal. I'll be out to check on him later."

"Don't worry about Peaceable." Aaron reached for his bridle. "It's my privilege to care for him."

Mahlon turned to Jake. "If you are willing to confess your sin of sloth—"

Jake jumped. Aubrey wasn't sure whether it was the word *sloth* or *confess* that had upset him.

"What?" Mahlon said. "You think because I'm injured I don't know what goes on around here? You think I don't know Aaron has been carrying your responsibilities as well as his—and doing them better?"

"But—"

Mahlon held up a hand. "No buts. As I said, if you will confess your sin of sloth to the congregation and the sins of temper and deceit, especially in relation to this incident, I will reconsider my decision. *If* I believe there is genuine repentance. Otherwise, you must leave." He turned and went into the house.

9

Aubrey followed Aaron as he led the horse into the barn. When she glanced back to see where Jake was, he had disappeared. *Good riddance.* "Will Peaceable be all right?"

"Physically, yeah. The injuries are superficial. The skin over the welts isn't split, and the cuts on his legs aren't deep." He sighed. "But I'm afraid it'll take him a while to trust anyone again."

"Peaceable was already mad at the world, wasn't he?" Aubrey didn't know much about horses, and she wasn't ashamed to admit it. That one generation removed from Amish life had made a huge difference, sort of like the second generation of an immigrant family not knowing much about the old country. Even so, she'd seen this one in action. "Poor baby." She reached toward him to offer a comforting pet.

Aaron put a hand out to stop her. "I wouldn't touch him right now. He's too upset. I wouldn't want you to get bitten."

She pulled her hand back. "Okay. I don't want to get bitten either. But you touch him."

"He knows me at least a little bit. He knows I've never been unkind to him." Aaron led him to a post with a clip on it. He attached Peaceable to it with a short lead.

Aubrey sat on a bale of hay and watched as Aaron washed Peaceable with cool water to remove the sweat and soothe the hurts, murmuring soothingly the whole time.

Peaceable moved uncertainly as Aaron worked, obviously afraid of further pain.

After he gently patted Peaceable dry, Aaron smeared salve on the welts and cuts. By the time he led the horse into a stall, Peaceable seemed as at ease as the unhappy horse ever did.

"Horse whisperer." Aubrey smiled. "I knew it."

After he'd firmly closed the stall half door, Aaron stood for a moment, studying Aubrey.

"What?" she asked.

"Ever ride in a sulky?"

She blinked and shook her head. Pictures of Peaceable rearing and throwing her out of the vehicle flashed through her head. She'd slide across the road and come to rest just in time for a car to run over her. Or she'd slide into a field recently topped with manure. Or the horse would step on her, leaving a permanent horseshoe mark on her cheek or her forehead or her neck. She swallowed against the imagined pressure.

He seemed to read her mind. "I don't mean Peaceable. He's down for the night."

"Okay. That's good."

"Say I did want to use him," Aaron said, his tone challenging. "You don't trust me to control him?"

"Um . . ." How could she say no without insulting him?

Aaron quirked an eyebrow at her. "Where's your adventurous spirit?"

What adventurous spirit? "I left it in New Jersey. Maybe I'm just too old for risk." She'd risked with Ethan and look how that had turned out.

"When you're eighty-five and wobbly on your feet, you can say that. Not now." He reached out a hand and pulled her up. "Wait here while I get the horse."

He walked out the rear of the barn, leaving her in the barn's dim interior. She was glad all the years of visiting her mom's family had inured her to the smells of livestock. *Pungent* barely covered it.

A little brown hen dropped down from her perch at the edge of the haymow and raced down the middle of the aisle between stalls. She came to rest at Aubrey's feet where she pecked expectantly at Aubrey's shoe.

Delighted by the little creature, Aubrey knelt and held out a hand. "I don't have any food, you cute little thing. Sorry. I didn't know you were here."

The hen moved under her hand and clucked.

"You want petting? That I can do." She ran her hand down the soft feathers. A soft gurgle of contentment slid out of the little hen, and she rubbed her cheek against Aubrey's hand. Aubrey took the hint and scratched there. The bird's eyes slid shut in delight.

Aaron walked in with Starry Night on a lead and laughed when he saw Aubrey with the hen now sitting in her lap. "So Missy's added you to her circle of admirers."

Aubrey ran her hand down the feathered back. "She's adorable."

"The children love her. Somehow I don't think she'll end up on their dinner table like the rest of the hens or the turkey out there." He nodded toward the fenced patch with all the animals.

Peaceable peered over the edge of his stall's half door. He ignored Starry Night but spotted the little hen. His lip curled and he snorted. Aubrey felt Missy stiffen. The hen turned to the great beast looming several feet over her head, her whole demeanor going from happy lady enjoying attention to outraged damsel whose space had been invaded. With a defiant squawk she jumped out of Aubrey's lap and marched out of the barn. Peaceable shook his head and disappeared back into his stall. Starry Night seemed to have missed the whole interaction.

"Territorial struggles," Aaron said as he slipped the bridle over Starry Night's head.

"Their animosity makes Jake versus the world seem like a T-ball competition."

Aaron worked quickly, attaching the horse to the sulky. Then he handed Aubrey up and climbed in after her. The two of them were a tight squeeze on the narrow seat, which forced them to sit with her shoulder tucked behind his. Try as she might, she couldn't consider it a hardship.

He flicked the reins, and with a toss of his head, Starry Night left the barn. He seemed eager for a run, but Aaron kept a tight hold on the reins to control his pace.

"So tell me about New Jersey," he said as they moved onto the road where they progressed at a slow but steady walk. It was a beautiful evening, the golden hour washing everything in brilliant color. Aubrey found herself finally relaxing, the confrontation with Jake receding as they rolled on.

They passed an Amish neighbor, and Aubrey was tickled to see a little boy seated in a yellow plastic car with a red roof, propelling himself around the driveway. If only a little car like that would satisfy Asa and Ben. Not that they'd fit in it.

As they moved ever so slowly down the road, Aubrey understood the lure of Amish taxis. Going somewhere in a buggy took forever—which her mom said was the idea. Buggies kept everyone close to home.

Aaron glanced over at her. "New Jersey," he prompted. "What caused you to leave your adventurous spirit there?"

Aubrey took a deep breath as she tried to figure how to explain Ethan without sounding a fool—if she even wanted to mention him at all.

Aaron noted her hesitation. "That bad, huh?"

She frowned, suddenly angry for no reason she could discern.

He grinned at her expression. "It must be a doozy of a story."

Her anger drained away. It wasn't Aaron she was mad at. It was herself. And Ethan. She was definitely still mad at Ethan.

"Why don't you start with his name?"

"His name was Ethan Sharpe."

After a moment of silence, Aaron said, "And?"

"And I was an idiot." She felt herself flushing.

"Who of us hasn't been an idiot about a member of the opposite sex?"

"Yeah, well, some of us are bigger idiots than others." So whom had Aaron been an idiot over? Was she, whoever she was, the reason he was still single?

"Was he handsome?"

"Handsome enough." It was an understatement. Her heart had skipped the first time she'd seen him. "His big talent was laying on the charm. He oozed it. And I fell for it." She stared at the sky. "As I said, I was an idiot."

"I doubt that. You seem pretty intelligent to me, though sometimes our judgment gets clouded in matters of the heart. So what did he do? Ditch you for someone else?"

"If only."

Aaron whistled. "There's worse?"

"He disappeared."

"You mean he just left, maybe twisting the knife so charmingly that you ended up feeling sorry for his pain?"

"I did *not* feel sorry for him." She heard the hardness in her voice, but Aaron didn't know the whole story.

"Then you felt sorry for yourself?"

She glared at him. That hit much too close to home. "You're nosy."

He shrugged. "About people I like."

She stared at him.

Again he gave her that grin. "That was a compliment, you know."

"I'm supposed to be impressed because you like me?"

"Seems reasonable to me."

To her too. Wonderful, in fact. But she wasn't about to be taken in that easily again, especially by an unavailable Amish man. "Great. Another charmer."

He sat up straighter. "You think I'm a charmer? You just made my day."

"Amish men aren't allowed to be charming." Which was as foolish a statement as she'd ever made. "Rather they aren't allowed to be happy they're charming. It's prideful, and we all know the middle letter in *pride* is that dangerous pronoun *I*."

He laughed. "Where did you hear that one?"

"My Amish aunt Edna."

"You have Amish family?"

"Lots of them." She stiffened as a car drove up behind them. She was used to being the person in the car, not the Amish conveyance. The car zoomed around, the breeze of its passing blowing her hair. "That was weird."

"I'd say unnerving. Easy, Starry. Easy, fella."

"I'd have thought you were used to cars passing."

"I'm not, especially with a horse in training. It's nerve-racking."

"Was traffic this bad where you lived?"

"No. The area is less populated."

"You miss home?"

"Sure. Don't we always miss home when we're away, at least if we love our families?"

"I'm glad to hear you love your family." A safe topic. Anything but Ethan. "I love mine too." This reminded her of something she'd been meaning to ask him. "You never speak Pennsylvania Dutch. How come?"

He frowned. "Loving my family makes you question my speech?"

"An Amish boy should speak Dutch."

He shrugged. "Not Iowa Amish guys."

"Why not?"

"Most Amish in Iowa have Swiss-German heritage, which is a different dialect, enough that you wouldn't understand me if I spoke it. Therefore I limp along in English."

She gave a snort, not at all a ladylike sound. "I must say you limp along quite well."

He grinned, and she realized with alarm that she was becoming addicted to that smile. "Do you like being Amish?" She bit her lip. Now who was being nosy? She was afraid what she was really asking was whether he was willing *not* to be Amish.

But he chuckled. "Now there's a question out of the blue. Do you like being English?"

"I do. I know I could never be Amish." That was her side of their impossible situation, if there was a *their*. "I bet you'd make a good English person."

He gazed at her sharply. "Why do you say that?"

Why *had* she said it? Because he was like a regular guy from her world? Because he talked to her easily? Because she was much too attracted to him? "I don't know. Maybe because you seem normal—no, that's not what I mean. Of course you're normal."

"There's a relief."

"Sometimes I feel there's an invisible barrier between the Amish and us English, and I don't feel it with you." She shrugged, hoping he wouldn't look over and see her red face. "That's the best I can do, and I don't mean to be insulting."

"I know," he said quietly, studying Starry Night's back. "Time to go back to the farm. It's getting dark." He turned them and headed back toward the Eabys'.

"I'm sorry," she said. "I don't think I've been this rude since—well, maybe ever."

"I don't think you were rude at all." He grinned at her. "I recognize another compliment when I hear one. Not only am I charming, I'm also normal."

She peeked at him to see how sarcastic he was being, and their eyes locked.

"And I like compliments coming from you," he said, his voice low.

For a moment she couldn't breathe. She felt scared of her feelings and of what she saw in his eyes. *Make that terrified.*

He turned back to the road. "If that makes me prideful, then guilty as charged."

When she finally managed another lungful of air, she went for sarcasm to defuse the atmosphere. "You like compliments so much you obviously missed all the lessons at church on the evils of pride and the giving up of self." *Uffgevva* her mother called it—the yielding of individual interests and desires to the community for the good of the community.

He laughed, not the least offended. "Cheer up. We Pennsylvania charmers are much nicer than New Jersey charmers."

"Yeah, well, that makes me feel great. Besides, you're not even from Pennsylvania."

When he laughed, she couldn't help but join him.

You're on dangerous ground here, Aubrey.

10

When the doorbell sounded at her apartment that evening, Aubrey went unsuspectingly to the door, her honey-colored cocker spaniel prancing at her feet.

"Someone to see you, Buster?" She peeked out the little fish-eye and saw a distorted image of a wild-eyed Bekka.

Oh no. Aubrey had no idea what this could be about, but she knew it couldn't be good. She rested her head against the door. Buster sat at her feet and cocked his head to one side in question. To him, this was where she was supposed to open the door so he could check out whoever was on the other side of it.

She had been happily enjoying the memories of her ride with Aaron, Buster sitting beside her on the couch, his head in her lap as she gave him a good ear rub. She'd been reliving the feel of Aaron's strong shoulder pressed to hers, the warmth in his eyes when he smiled at her. Whatever Bekka wanted, one thing was certain: she would not keep the glow going. Taking a deep breath, Aubrey opened the door to her cousin.

Bekka pushed her way in, dragging a black trash bag behind her. Buster barked, then darted away before he was bowled over by the bag. When Bekka came to a stop, he looked from her to the mysterious bag to her again. He gave a little bark.

"Hello, dog. I don't have anything for you." Bekka turned to Aubrey. "I'm moving in."

Aubrey eyed the girl. *Really? Whatever happened to asking?* At least if Bekka had asked, she'd have had a chance to say no. Who would ever choose to give up the healing peace and quiet of a solitary life for the emotional storm called Bekka and the endless family complications that came with her? She could hear again the frost in Rachel's single word: *Don't.*

Or—scary thought—was God asking her to practice her own kind of Uffgevva? The idea made her stomach drop but also softened her voice. "What happened, kiddo?"

"I can't stand it there any longer!"

"I know. But what happened?"

"They had a quilting at the house today. I was supposed to participate, but I hate quilting. I hate all needlework. I wanted to stay in my room and read. I got the most wonderful books on astronomy and the universe at the library, and I wanted to read them." Her face lit up. "You should see the pictures of supernovas and the Martian moon—the colors are beautiful! And the Crab Nebula. And you wouldn't believe Supernova 1987A!"

Aubrey thought she was probably right, whatever Supernova 1987A was.

"It has a red center and ring of blue—I don't know, maybe stars. They remind me of a diamond bracelet in the picture. They wouldn't let me read the book and find out!"

"They made you go quilt." Poor Bekka. Her family was perfectly nice, but they'd never understand this kind of passion for learning.

"My father said I had to leave my books and be with the women. He came to my room and took them away! He said he was taking them back to the library, and they should stay there." She glared at Aubrey with eyes that sparkled with angry tears. "Can you believe it?"

Aubrey frowned. Not a wise move on Uncle Eli's part in her opinion, but Bekka probably scared her parents with her excitement over English things.

Bekka unpinned her Kapp and twisted it in her hands. She glared at it. "Then the bishop came over this evening to talk to me about my attitude."

"Oh, Bekka. I'm sorry." Such authority was intimidating.

"I'm not questioning anything." Bekka flung her arms wide. "I look at the sky at night and I know Gott is there. I study those books about the universe, and I know He must have created such wonders. Isn't that what matters?"

"It's certainly a good starting place," Aubrey said.

"I asked my father to show the books to the bishop so he could see that they aren't dangerous. I'm just interested in different things than most of the women we know. The bishop saw the amazing pictures and told me the heavens belong to the Lord." Bekka frowned in confusion. "Of course they do. I know that. But he said I shouldn't question what is too great for me to understand."

She began pacing as she had at Mammi's party. "The bishop said that if my father says no more books, then no more books. He pointed his bony old finger at me and reminded me that the Bible says, 'Children, obey your parents.'" Her eyes were desperate. "But I'm not a child anymore!"

Poor Bekka. Aubrey wrapped her arms around the girl in a hug. Bekka let her hold her for a moment, then stiffened and moved away. She grabbed her black bag. Buster, who had been poking it with his nose as he tried to figure out what it was, dashed under the table in the eating area.

"So here I am," Bekka said. "Where do you want me?"

"Honey, they only want what they think is best for you. They love you."

"I know, and I love them. It'd all be so much easier if I didn't. I could do whatever I wanted and not care. But how do they know what's best for me? *I* don't even know!" She collapsed on the sofa, tears spilling down her cheeks.

Aubrey sat beside her, her heart hurting for the miserable girl. "Bekka, you are a questioner. Your mom and dad aren't."

"I am. I know that. Is that so bad?"

"I don't think it is, but it scares them. They're afraid they're going to lose you."

"Like Mammi lost your mother. I know. They keep telling me that. She's their example of someone who lost her way. But your mom isn't lost."

"You're right. She isn't. But she's also not what your parents consider *found*."

"Nobody gives her trouble. They accept her."

"That's true now. But they were all very upset when she left. She told me they had the bishop over and everything. It was hard for all of them. I know she and Mammi are close now, but they have to work at it. There is and always will be a barrier between them. Mom stepped outside their understanding of what God asks of His people."

Bekka snorted. "So she made the mistake of thinking for herself."

"It's a lot more complicated than that."

"I think for myself. I don't understand how they can accept whatever they're told so completely. No questions. No curiosity. The *Ordnung* says it, so it must be true. The bishop says it, so it must be true. I don't understand why questions are wrong! The bishop's only a man and the Ordnung changes from district to district."

"And they don't understand how you can doubt what to them is right and reasonable. Their whole lives they've been taught to yield to authority—God's and their leaders'—and that's what they do."

"And I can't." Bekka sighed. "I wish I could. I wish I could be like Louisa, who can't wait to be married and a mother. She's desperate to have her own kitchen. She loved the quilting this afternoon, especially since the quilt was being made for her."

Aubrey felt immense sympathy for Bekka. It was difficult to be out of step with a community that had firmly established patterns that gave it cohesion and meaning. The keeping of those patterns led to salvation, and stepping aside was heresy. It wasn't so much supernovas that bothered Aunt Susie and Uncle Eli. It was the fear of Bekka falling from God's favor.

Bekka gathered Buster into her lap. "So I've got to stay with you."

"You've decided not to be Amish?" Aubrey knew she and her mother would get the blame for this decision.

"No, I haven't decided yet. But it'll be easier to choose from here because I won't be angry all the time." She reached over Buster and pulled a purple T-shirt from the black plastic bag. "One of the kids where I work gave this to me for my birthday as a sort of challenge. She told me to either find the courage to wear it, or stop whining and give it away. I love it and I want to wear it. You can take me shopping so I can get jeans to go with it."

The financial cost of Bekka's adventures in the English world began to occur to Aubrey. "I'm supposed to clothe you?"

"I make money at my job." Bekka worked at a nursery not far from the family farm. In an industry where most employees were seasonal, she was one of the few who worked all year. "You can take me shopping in your car, but I'll buy my clothes."

"How much do you make?"

She named a figure that would not go far, even at a discount store.

"And," Bekka said as if she was proud she'd figured it out, "you can drop me at work on your way to work every morning and pick me up on your way home."

But what if Aubrey wanted to go riding in a sulky with a handsome and charming Amish man? She shook her head. "Bekka, I only have one bedroom."

Bekka shrugged. "I'll sleep on the sofa, at least until you get a two-bedroom apartment."

Aubrey shook her head. "I'm not getting a bigger apartment."

"Why not?"

"I can't afford it."

"But you've got a good job."

She did, but how could she make a girl who had never wanted for anything understand? Bekka lived in a home where food and clothing appeared as a matter of course. She gave the money she earned to her father, but it hadn't dawned on her that her small income did not meet the cost of her upkeep. It would meet her needs even less in the English world largely because the Amish and English definitions of *need* differed as widely as their modes of transportation.

Bekka gaped at her. "You don't want to help me."

"It's not that simple."

"You're afraid everyone will get mad at you."

"Well, that's a given."

The girl waved a hand. "You don't have to worry. I'll tell them it's all my fault. I'll tell them I had to fight you to get you to help me."

If only convincing people could be that easy. But it wasn't the only consideration. Aubrey sighed. "I'm broke, Bekka. I can't afford to help anyone."

Bekka looked around the room, her face skeptical. Aubrey followed her gaze. Flat-screen TV. Nice cushy furniture in cream and rust. A faux Oriental rug in cream, rust, and black. Pretty pictures, but they were all from before Ethan had ruined her.

Aubrey understood that Bekka saw pretty things and thought her flush with money. If she only knew. "All bought before I became stupid."

Bekka eyed her. "A person can't *become* stupid."

Aubrey's wry smile felt more than slightly sour. "I'm so broke I had to live with my parents when I first came home. When we found this little apartment, they put the money down for me. I'm paying rent, I'm paying on my car, I'm paying them back, and I'm paying on a loan I took out back when I was an idiot."

It took a minute, but Bekka asked, "What was his name?"

Being stupid over a man must be cross-cultural. "Ethan."

"Handsome?"

"Very."

"Did he rob you or something? Is that why you can't afford a bigger apartment?"

"Sort of." Aubrey took a deep breath. It would be embarrassing, but Bekka needed to understand.

Bekka seemed intrigued. "This sounds like it might be an interesting story. Can I go get a drink first? Do you have anything fizzy?"

"There's ginger ale in the fridge. Can you bring me a glass too?" Aubrey was grateful for the short reprieve. Who knew? Maybe it would feel good to talk about this with someone.

Even Bekka.

The young woman jumped up and raced toward the kitchen. Aubrey picked up Buster and petted him as she took herself back through the ugly events.

He'd conned her.

And he'd been so good at it. He'd showered her with attention, making her feel like the most wonderful woman in the world. He'd spent all his free time with her for more than six months, taking her to expensive restaurants and slouching on her sofa with her as they watched Sunday-afternoon football. "How did I ever live without you?" he would say as he kissed her.

She'd met him at the singles group at her church. She was standing with a couple of girlfriends, drinking coffee, when he approached them, a bottle of water in his hand.

"Three beautiful ladies! How lucky can a guy get?" He saluted them with his bottle and offered his hand to shake, apparently trying to show that he not only appreciated their appearances but also respected them as individuals. "I'm Ethan Sharpe, new to town and this church." He grinned at the three of them with a twinkle in his eye that removed any hint he might be a wolf on the prowl. "I think I've found a home."

In no time he had them all laughing and their interest piqued. A charming single guy who was intelligent and handsome, well-dressed and socially adept? And he talked about the Lord as if they were good friends. A man like that didn't come along every day.

It was only much later when she reflected on that day that she realized he'd carefully questioned the three of them about what they did for a living. Alice was an administrative assistant, and Jocelyn, a librarian. She was a physical therapist. He had zeroed in on her because he judged she had the highest income. She had never suspected any ulterior motive at the time—she'd been too pleased he'd chosen her. Every day she had thanked God she had finally met a man she could trust and respect.

He had slipped in the part about his wonderful business opportunity so skillfully that she never questioned a thing. "I'm so excited about the possibilities," he'd said. "Can you believe it? I have to pinch myself." He made it sound so reasonable, so perfect.

"And I convinced the guys to let you in on it too. They didn't want to open the opportunity to anyone else, but I told them how special you are." She would have the chance of a lifetime, he said. He'd invest her money for her in this sure thing, and there'd be a nice income stream for years, maybe forever. She'd be like the people who bought into Coca-Cola at the beginning, or Microsoft, or Amazon. When he accepted the $5,000 in savings she'd managed to accumulate and the $50,000 loan she'd taken out to invest in his dream, he'd gushed with excitement. "You are absolutely amazing! We'll watch this amazing thing unfold together."

It was only later that she realized he'd never shown her a business plan—and she'd never asked. He'd never introduced her to any of the other men he claimed to be working with. He'd also never said the words *love* or *marriage*. She'd just heard them in her head because she was so infatuated.

"Sweetheart, how could I ever live without you?" became "We'll be together forever in our own little cottage with a picket fence and a two-car garage and a pool in the backyard. We'll have the matching wedding rings and two or three kids and a dog and a cat." A month before she gave him the money, he'd actually bought her the dog—her beloved cocker spaniel.

How many tears had she shed in Buster's soft fur over the past year? Sometimes she wondered if she'd ever regain her self-respect.

11

When Aubrey finished telling Bekka an abbreviated version of her pathetic tale, Bekka studied her. "I always thought you were the smart one. I mean, you went to college on scholarships and you've got a couple of degrees."

"Not smart. Just educated."

"There's a difference?"

"A big one."

"Huh," Bekka said thoughtfully. "I might not be educated, but I'm smart. And I have common sense. Is there a difference between common sense and smart?"

"That's an interesting question. What do you think?"

"I think there is. And because I have both, I think it's foolish to try and make me like things like sewing and cooking but tell me I can't like things like the universe."

"Doesn't your Rumspringa give you the freedom you want while you try and make up your mind about your future? Isn't that its purpose?"

"Yeah, but even so, I'm being pressured to get baptized and join the church. And marry. And I don't want to!" The last was a wail.

Aubrey wasn't sure what to say to the girl. Her own mother and father were so careful to avoid offending the family. Helping Bekka leave would certainly create ill feelings. She could imagine Mammi's hurt and Aunt Edna's criticisms. She heard again Rachel's scathing "Don't."

But she couldn't turn her back on Bekka either. The girl was genuinely hurting.

Bekka flung her arms wide. "I just need to be free!"

Aubrey mentally rolled her eyes at the drama. "Honey, you're smart enough to know no one's free. Everyone answers to someone, and we all answer to God."

Bekka shrugged. "Maybe I'll solve all my problems and marry some rich English guy."

Aubrey couldn't help a laugh. "I hate to break it to you, but there aren't that many rich English guys just waiting for ex-Amish girls to come along."

"A girl can dream."

Like she used to dream about Ethan. "Where does your mother think you are?"

Bekka was suddenly the picture of guilt. Aubrey was immediately reminded of the time her dog had chewed up her favorite slippers.

"Bekka! You mean she's home worrying about you?"

"We had a fight."

"About?"

Bekka's chin came up defiantly, and for a moment Aubrey thought she wasn't going to answer. Then she said, "Carter Betancourt."

"English?" Stupid question. Of course he was English with a name like that. And Aubrey realized that though there was no denying the girl was not the typical Amish young woman and that made life hard for her, Carter was the real reason for tonight's dramatics. A disquieting thought hit Aubrey. Was Bekka thinking of Carter with her comment about marrying a rich English guy?

"He's wonderful!" Bekka's face took on a besotted expression.

Of course he was. "Where did you meet him?" Certainly not in the closely monitored circle of the Amish community.

"At the nursery."

"He works there?"

Bekka scratched Buster under his chin. "He came in a couple of months ago because his mother sent him for purple pansies. She needed more. I helped him find what he needed, and he just started talking." She rested her cheek on Buster's head. "He asked me out."

Aubrey knew that day at the nursery, Carter had seen the lovely Amish girl instead of the unhappy and extremely complicated rebel. "So you went with him?"

"I met him at the end of the lane, and he took me to the gas station so I could change into some English clothes he borrowed from his sister."

Aubrey tried to imagine going into the restroom as one person and coming out as another. "I don't know if I like a guy who helps you deceive your parents. And I definitely don't like you letting your mother worry about you all night. Come on." Aubrey rose, grabbed her purse, and moved to the door. Buster followed hopefully, his stump of a tail wagging.

"Where are we going?"

"I'm taking you home."

Bekka leaped to her feet. "No! Please, no!"

Aubrey held out her hand. "Stop."

Bekka fell silent, but her face was a thundercloud.

"I will not disrespect your parents by letting them worry about you. And neither should you."

The thundercloud gave way to guilt. "You can go and tell them where I am. I-I'll just wait here." Her eyes fell on the flat-screen. "I'll watch something on TV while I wait for you to come back."

Aubrey paused with her hand on the doorknob. "I didn't realize you were a coward."

The thundercloud reappeared. "I am not a coward!"

"Then be brave enough to do this the right way, Bekka. My mother didn't sneak off and not tell Mammi where she was going. She told her she was visiting an English church with one of the girls at work. She told her when she wanted to stop going to Amish services. Mammi always knew exactly what Mom was doing. Your mother and father deserve the same consideration."

Bekka sighed as if her world had collapsed.

"Come on. Buster and I will take you home. Which makes me wonder—how did you get here?"

"Carter."

Big surprise there.

Bekka gave it one last try. "Please, Aubrey. Let me—"

"No way, kiddo. You're going home. But would you like to come visit Saturday, spend the night, then go to church with us—Mom, Dad, Scott, and me—and spend the day? I'll take you home sometime Sunday."

The girl's face cleared. "Really? I'll come. I'll come! Can Carter come too?"

Aubrey opened the door. "Don't push it." She started down the hall, Buster at her heels, wondering what she had gotten herself into.

Thursday passed without a visit from Bekka, thank goodness, and then it was Friday and time for a visit with Mahlon and Miriam.

As Aubrey approached the farm, she saw Asa and Ben riding along the side of the road on their scooters. They sported their safety vests, the ones they wore as they went to and from school.

The scooters always made Aubrey think of bicycles because of the size of the wheels, but instead of pedals and chain midway up the wheels, a footboard was inches off the street. Bicycles were as verboten locally as electricity from the power company and telephones in the house.

As she watched, Asa dropped his scooter and dashed into a field. She slowed to a stop and lowered her window in time to hear Ben call, "Did you find him?"

Asa reappeared, shaking his head. "I don't know what I saw, but it wasn't him." He picked up his scooter, then paused when he saw Aubrey.

The boys' faces were troubled. "What's wrong?" she asked.

Ben peered at the field. "Tom's missing. He got out somehow."

Did he mean Aaron's friend Trent? "What do you mean, he got out somehow?"

"I don't know," Asa said. "Every so often a hen escapes and wanders along the road. But Tom? He's too big to get under the fence. And he can't fly. Daed clipped his wings."

"You mean Tom the turkey? The big white bird?"

The boys nodded politely, though their expressions said, "Who else?" "He was in the yard last night, and he's gone today."

"Did someone steal him?"

The boys looked aghast at the idea. "Who would do that?"

Who indeed? The road was lined with Amish farms, people the Eabys knew well, went to church with regularly, socialized with. Aubrey had as much trouble imagining one of them grabbing Tom as the boys seemed to.

She didn't repeat her thought that the bird had been taken. Or suggest that it had been coyotes. She didn't want to upset them more than they already were.

"We have to keep searching," Asa said. He pushed off on his scooter, Ben following. Aubrey drove on thoughtfully. She worried they'd never find the bird.

She studied the enclosure of animals as she turned into the lane. The hens scratched for corn as usual, the miniature horses swished their tails to keep the flies off, and the goat stood on top of the shelter like a climber who'd just conquered Everest.

She studied the waist-high enclosure, trying to think like someone who wanted to take Tom. It was just regular woven-wire fencing, galvanized for protection against the weather, the kind anyone could buy at any hardware store. She had no idea how far into the ground the posts that supported it had been driven, but it was sturdy enough for its purpose because the animals it contained weren't bent on escape.

It wouldn't be hard to cut with wire cutters of any strength. The thief could have cut his way in and shooed out all the critters, but he hadn't done that. He'd probably just jumped the fence. But jumping back out with a huge bird in his arms? Even if the turkey were easy to catch—and she wasn't sure about that—lugging him off would have been a challenge. He was about as big as a medium-size dog, especially when he spread his tail.

Would he have come quietly or would he have fought his captor? It was a pretty safe bet that he wasn't a cuddler like Missy. So why not take a hen? Surely a hen would be easier to catch than a turkey, especially if she was sleeping on her roost. Also her beak and claws weren't as large and lethal as Tom's.

All of which made her wonder if he hadn't already been killed when he was carried off. A quick twist and his neck would be wrung.

Aaron came out of the barn as she was getting her bag from the back of her car. His face was grim. "You've heard our news?"

"I bumped into the boys on the road. Only Tom's missing?"

"Only Tom."

She studied him. "And you think the same thing I do."

He managed a small smile. "Aren't you the clever lady?"

"I like to think so." She mentally cringed. Had she just said that aloud?

But Aaron didn't seem to think any less of her, because he grinned. Her heart gave a traitorous flutter. *He's Amish, Aubrey. Amish.*

She pulled up the handle on her bag. "I understand why I jumped to my conclusion. I'm jaded from too much TV and too much news. You're not supposed to be suspicious. You're supposed to be kind and forgiving."

Aaron clapped his hand over his heart. "If only that were so. I must say you have a strange concept of what being Amish is like. You've read too many Amish novels."

"Probably." And there was Mom's family, who were careful to show only the best of Amish life when she was around.

He glanced at the house. "The bishop came to see Mahlon today."

"He's not in any trouble, is he?" she asked, alarmed.

Aaron shook his head. "They talked about Jake. Mahlon told the bishop about the turkey."

"How do you know?"

"They asked me some questions about Jake too."

Of course they did. Aaron had worked with him every day. "Do you know what they decided? What they're going to do?"

He spread his hands. "They're not going to do anything."

"They're not going to tell the police?"

"It's a missing turkey, Aubrey. Hardly a threat to the township."

"But they should know even if they can't or won't do anything."

"Neither the bishop nor Mahlon want to involve outsiders. They want to resolve the situation inside the community."

Us versus them. Aubrey sighed.

12

Trent ran a hand down the neck of the handsome palomino that belonged to one of the girls.

"You are one well-mannered lady, aren't you"—he glanced at the nameplate by the door—"Golden Girl?" He patted the horse, then put on her lead and walked her from her stall to the pasture behind the barn. When he opened the gate, Golden Girl trotted to the far end of the field and back, stopping beside the other two horses, who nickered in welcome.

Trent stood and watched them for a few minutes, resting his arms on the top rail of the white fence that edged the pasture, but he really didn't see them. Instead his father filled his thoughts. With this time alone had come a more balanced reaction to him. Even though the man was right about so many things, that Father-knows-best attitude irritated Trent. Still he had to admire him. He was a man of principle and purpose.

In many ways Trent found being his son hard, but he also realized what a privilege it was to be raised by a man of integrity. The problem arose when they didn't agree on those things about which his father felt there was no debate. The biggest of those things was Trent's future.

Trent shook his head. He was going to drive himself crazy with all the introspection. He pushed away from the fence and turned toward the house. He'd been here alone for a week now, setting his own schedule, eating and sleeping whenever he felt like it, watching

TV during the day, swimming in the middle of the night. He smiled at himself.

At first he'd loved the freedom from a schedule. There was something exhilarating about doing whatever he wanted whenever he wanted. One day he drove for hours just to watch how the local Amish community managed in the midst of so much tourism. He even went to the Amish attractions near Lancaster that were geared to inform tourists about the culture. He took a buggy ride with two young couples from New York City who couldn't imagine living without electricity.

"How do you make your morning coffee?" one of the men asked the driver.

"How do you dry your hair?" his wife countered.

Didn't they realize that everyone had managed before electricity? Visions of women with perpetually wet heads forced Trent to bite back a smile.

"No TV," said the other man. "No NFL. How do they keep up with their fantasy teams?"

"Come on, Ross," his wife said. "They don't have fantasy teams. They have peace."

If they only knew. With the little he knew about the Jake incident at the Eabys, Trent could have told them it wasn't all peace. There were still disappointing children and struggles to help them, just as among any group of people. There were illnesses and hard times, financial woes and personal disagreements. Wearing suspenders and Kapps didn't make life trouble free. It did not guarantee happiness.

Several days into his two weeks of relaxation, Trent grew so itchy with all the unclaimed time on his hands that he mowed the yard, loving the smell of the freshly cut grass. He watered the plants lining the walk and in the beds out front and in the garden out back. All flowers. No vegetables. He weeded. He deadheaded. He visited nurseries searching for flowers his mother might like.

Tuesday he'd discovered that most of the black-eyed Susans in the garden had been chewed down to the ground. How had that happened? Monday they had been fine—not yet tall so early in the season but not stunted.

Marauding rabbits, it turned out. He ended up spraying a vile-smelling liquid he found at the garden center on what remained of the flowers. To his great satisfaction, it seemed to be working. No more leaves had been chewed off, and there was a hint of new growth. He hoped that there would be more soon so he could present a garden on the mend when the family came home rather than a disaster that had occurred on his watch. The great cluster of Shasta daisies about to flower apparently did not interest the rabbits.

What surprised him was that he'd worked in the garden by choice, and he found it extremely satisfying. The garden had always been his mother's responsibility and joy, and he'd steered clear as much as he could manage. Now it gave purpose to his growing restlessness.

His father was a man of purpose and order, so much so it often drove Trent crazy, but he was learning he was a creature of habit too. He wasn't sure he was happy with that realization, but it appeared to be true. A week ago he would have shuddered at any similarity between his father and him, but now he had to wonder if maybe his father wasn't on to something.

Still the choices of how to live his life—how to work, where to work, what to believe—were his choices to make, not his father's.

Saturday morning he was up and had fed himself and the animals by six. The day stretched long. He sat and read until he felt it was a decent time to visit Aaron.

He walked back into the barn to collect what Aaron had requested he bring when he next visited. He tossed everything into the trunk and put down the top of the convertible. Today was perfect for driving with the sun and wind in his face. He also kept the car's air-conditioning on. His father would say that was a foolish idea, a waste of resources, but Trent loved the combination of nature's warmth and manmade chill.

What did Sally think about such things? He'd like to talk to her, the girl with the fantastic crinkly smile.

He cleared his throat. He might as well admit it. He wasn't visiting to check on Aaron or even to bring Aaron the items he'd asked to borrow. He was going to the Eabys' because he wanted to see Sally.

He turned into the lane and pulled to a halt beneath the big maple. He climbed from the car and went to the barn, calling for Aaron. Might as well make it look as if that were his purpose.

He didn't appear. Trent turned and walked to the house. Before he could even climb the stairs, the door opened and Sally appeared, followed by two little girls. She was listening carefully to something one girl was saying. Harper, he thought.

Sally was smiling the wonderful smile at the child.

Smile at me!

As if she heard him, she glanced up and their eyes met. "Oh!" She took a step back.

This time he was quick enough to smile instead of stand there like a fool. She hesitated a minute, then smiled back briefly before she dropped her gaze. Trent's heart stumbled for several seconds before righting itself.

"Did you want Aaron? I'm afraid he's over at the neighbor's. I'm not sure when he's returning."

"Oh, okay. I guess I'll come back later."

Before she could respond, the older child with her said, "I'm Anna." She had none of Sally's shyness. "And that's Harper."

"I fall down steps," Harper informed him. She pointed to the bruise on her forehead.

In spite of Harper's slight lisp and her Pennsylvania Dutch, Trent understood what she said. He answered in his own fractured Dutch. "Oh no. Have you recovered?"

Harper stared blankly.

He tried again. "Are you better?"

Harper smiled. "All better."

"We're going to weed," Anna said.

"Help Sally." Harper grabbed Sally's hand and walked to the edge of the stairs.

"While it's still cool." Anna started down the steps, pulling Sally along by her other hand.

Trent stepped back to give them room so shy Sally wouldn't feel threatened. "I'm just going to check on Peaceable for a minute."

Sally sent him a vague smile, then concentrated on the girls again.

Trent turned and walked through the barn to the back pasture. The two horses he was familiar with and a new one he hadn't seen before came over to investigate him. He greeted each one with gentle words and neck rubs. Satisfied, they wandered away and were soon grazing.

Peaceable stood at the far end of the field, alone as usual. Trent skirted the fence until he reached the cantankerous animal. From what he could see, the welts had disappeared, and his coat was smooth. His legs had recovered too. Yet, healthy as he appeared, somehow his whole body seemed to droop with despondency.

"It doesn't have to be as bad as you think," Trent told him. "Sometimes you just have to go along with the plan."

Peaceable eyed him as if he didn't believe a word.

Feeling sad for the horse, Trent walked back the way he'd come. *Sometimes you just have to go along with the plan.* Was he talking to himself or Peaceable?

He turned and shouted, "Don't give in, boy! Don't give in."

When he walked out of the barn, he saw Sally and the girls working in the garden. Sally was showing them which green things were weeds. He stood in the barn door and watched. She was so good with the little girls.

Miriam came onto the porch and called to Sally, "Can you come here a minute?"

"Of course." She turned to the girls. "Stay here. I need to see what your mother wants."

"We'll stay right here," Anna promised.

Sally smiled at the child, brushed her hands off on her skirt, and headed for Miriam. Anna and Harper watched her go. Then they crouched and got to work.

Sally caught Trent watching her and frowned. He smiled and she gave him a little nod in return. He swallowed his disappointment. No crinkly-eyed smile for him that time.

It occurred to him that she had to come back to the little girls again, so he wandered over to them.

"I'm impressed that you're working so hard."

They smiled up at him for a moment, then went back to their task. Then he saw the pile of weeds they had just pulled. *Uh-oh.*

He knelt. "Um, where did you learn to weed?" Hopefully not from Sally or their mother.

"We kept the pretty leaves," Anna explained.

"Pretty." Harper touched the green pile.

They'd left the ragweed in the ground. In a small pile withering under the hot sun were more than two dozen young zinnias, little more than leaves on six-inch stems, not even the beginnings of a bud visible to encourage the girls to leave them alone.

"I think you can pull this one too." He touched the ragweed, also about six inches high.

"It's a weed?" Anna asked

"Yes. It grows tall and makes people sneeze."

"It didn't make me sneeze."

"Not yet. Not until it grows up."

She reached for some young dahlias. "These too? They have pretty leaves. Do pretty leaves mean bad?"

Trent put out a hand to save the bloomless dahlias. "They're good guys. They will have pretty flowers soon."

Anna stared at the plants around her, all growing from seed and still young. "How do you know the good ones from the bad?"

"You learn."

"How about that?" She pointed to streamers of spurge creeping along at the edge of the lawn.

"Bad. You can pull that."

Anna grabbed it and tugged. "It's stuck."

"We probably need a trowel to loosen the dirt around it then."

A shadow fell over them—Sally.

Trent stood quickly. "We were just talking weeds."

Harper pointed to the ragweed. "Bad."

Anna pointed sadly to the dying zinnias. "I'm sorry. We thought the pretty one was good and these were bad."

Harper grinned. "I helped."

Trent recognized an opportunity when he saw one. "I can take you to the nursery over on 10 so you can get more zinnias." He noticed another pile of sun-dried leaves that he recognized as young snapdragons and ageratum. How had they pulled so much so fast?

Sally examined the scalped segment of garden and sighed.

"I know you can go in the buggy," Trent said, "but I've got my car right here. Let me take you."

"And me?" Harper asked. "And Ben and Asa and Mahlon? And Anna?"

"I was thinking just you gardening ladies, if that's all right." He was glad his imperfect Pennsylvania Dutch seemed to be understood.

"All right." Harper began walking to the car. She stopped and glanced over her shoulder. "You talk funny."

Well, that put him in his place.

"What do you say? The garden center?" He gazed hopefully at Sally, who was obviously torn.

After hesitating for several seconds, she nodded. "Let me tell Miriam."

Trent felt his heart lift. "I'll get the girls buckled in."

Sally disappeared into the house and Trent went to the car with Anna walking beside him.

"Harper's right. You do talk funny," she said.

"I do. I'm sorry. Can you still understand me?"

"Sort of. Enough."

He opened the back door and the girls climbed in. Trent wasn't certain what the law was about kid seats, but he knew he had to at least secure the girls. If they were supposed to have boosters or something, he couldn't provide that. Since they were only going about three miles, hopefully they'd be okay. It took some fiddling, but eventually both girls had seat belts on and the chest restraints weren't slapping them in the face.

"We don't wear these." Harper pulled at her belt. "I don't like it. Take it off."

"English people wear them. They keep us safe in this English car. I'll be wearing one and so will Sally."

Harper clearly wasn't happy, but authority had spoken. She settled.

Sally came out and climbed into the car. Without a word she fastened her seat belt. She glanced at him as he buckled up. She patted the leather seat. "Pretty fancy for an Amish taxi." And she smiled.

The ride to the nursery took less than five minutes, but it was time with Sally. At the nursery he followed her and the girls from greenhouse to greenhouse.

"These!" Harper pointed, only to change her mind as she saw another cluster of bright blooms. "No, these!"

"We're going to get what got pulled." Sally spoke softly, but the girls didn't argue. They bought a flat of mixed snapdragons with some of the plants in bloom, another of purple clusters of ageratum, and two of zinnias.

As they walked around the nursery, Trent noted an abundance of common bedding flowers, especially petunias, geraniums, and impatiens. There were some others like the ones Sally bought, but not many. There were no black-eyed Susans or Shasta daisies, both of which were staples in his mother's garden. He wondered what the market would be for more-unusual flowers.

They were back at the farm much too soon for Trent's taste. He carried the flats to the garden. "Want me to help you plant them?"

Sally met his gaze, and he thought he saw both sadness and determination in her eyes. "No, denke. It's been too much already."

Trent understood. He wished he could go to church with her tomorrow. Not that he could sit with her or anything. She'd be in the women's section and he'd be in the men's, but he'd know she was there. The service was being held at the farm just down the road. He'd seen the bench wagon in the front yard. But a man in English clothes would not be welcome, and he shouldn't push it.

13

"I want a bikini." Bekka held up a hanger with tiny scraps of fabric somehow attached.

Aubrey immediately pictured Aunt Susie's horror if she ever knew her daughter was wearing such a garment. "Absolutely not."

"But it's so cute."

Bekka had been in Aubrey's care for half an hour, and already a headache was brewing. "I promised your mother I'd take care of you. Getting you a bikini is not her or my idea of doing that."

"But you said we're going swimming in your parents' pool."

"We are."

"So I need this." She waved the bikini.

"We're getting a nice one-piece. You are going to be exposing skin that's never seen the light of day. We are not exposing *that* much."

"You're no fun."

"Would you rather swim in your dress?"

Bekka was still pouting when they paid for a sleek black suit with white piping. Once they were in the car, she said, "Carter thinks I should have gotten a two-piece."

"How does Carter even know?"

Bekka held up an expensive, top-of-the-line smartphone.

Aubrey frowned. If she couldn't afford one, how did Bekka manage? The answer was a no-brainer. "Carter?"

Bekka just smiled and slipped it into her pocket.

"Do your parents know you have it?"

"What do you think?" Bekka asked slyly. "And if you're wondering how I keep it working, I charge it at work."

And if her parents ever found the phone, they'd assume it was from Aubrey.

"I promise I won't try to convince her of anything," she'd promised Aunt Susie and Uncle Eli, who were not excited about the overnight. If they found the phone, they'd be convinced Aubrey had lied.

"Bekka, you may think of all this as your running around, so keeping things from your parents is okay. But I have a problem with all the secrecy. I want to help you, but I want to do things honorably. I understand your need to stretch and question, but I won't help you do it behind your parents' backs."

"I'm not giving up Carter." No mule had ever been so stubborn.

"Then he's a topic best avoided for the weekend."

At Aubrey's parents' house, the girls changed into their bathing suits. To Aubrey's relief, the kid clearly felt uncomfortable even in the more modest suit. There was still some Amish under that brazen act.

Aubrey handed her the sunscreen. "Slather this all over you, everywhere you can reach. When you're finished, I'll do your back. I don't want you getting all sunburned. Put it in your bag with the other things you want and take it out back with you. You'll need to reapply every so often, especially if you're in the water."

When they were at the back door ready to go into the yard, Bekka stopped. She hugged her towel to her chest. "There are men out there."

"My father and my brother, who are also your uncle and your cousin. You will never find anyone safer."

"And who's that girl? She's wearing a two-piece."

"Her name's Maddie and she's Scott's girlfriend. She's also older than you and English."

"He gets to bring his girlfriend, and I can't bring my boyfriend?" The pout reappeared at the unfairness.

Aubrey gave her a push toward the door. "For one thing, he's twenty-five and not sneaking around with her."

"That's two things. I'm calling Carter and telling him to come over."

"He's not invited, Bekka. Mom and Dad only invited you and me." After a little begging on Aubrey's part. She wanted all the help she could get with Bekka.

Bekka pawed through her bag. "Where is it?" She dumped everything on the kitchen table.

"Where's what?"

"My phone. It's missing!"

"Don't worry about it. You're here to spend time with us, not bury your face in your phone. We'll find it later."

"You took it, didn't you?" She pointed her finger. "You hid it! You can't do that! That's theft. I'll call 911."

"What?" Aubrey pushed down the anger she felt at the accusation. "I did not take your phone."

"Of course you did. It's not here. You stole my phone!"

It's important to her, Aubrey reminded herself. *It's a gift from Carter.* Still, the girl was out of line. "You want to go home, Bekka? Watch yourself or that's what will happen."

"Why are you so mean?" Bekka whined. "You're supposed to be on my side."

"I'm not being mean, and I *am* on your side. But that doesn't mean I will tolerate just anything from you." Aubrey made her voice as calm as she could. "You will not speak to me like that or accuse me of stealing from you. You may explore your options respectfully, or you won't explore them at all. Do you understand?" Each word, each syllable was slow and deliberate.

Bekka deflated immediately. "I didn't mean anything by it. I just don't know where my phone is."

"I will help you find it later. Now get out there and have fun before I throw you in the car and take you back where you came from. Remember you're only here out of the kindness of my heart. And don't forget to thank Mom for having us."

Within minutes Bekka was in the water, laughing, splashing, and playing catch with Scott and Maddie.

Mom patted Aubrey's hand. "You can do this, honey."

"She called me a thief. She accused me of taking something she's not supposed to have in the first place."

"She's confused and upset and unsure. Lashing out is how she covers it. Trust me, I remember how that felt."

"Well, pray for me. I've got thirty-plus hours to go." And she plunged into the pool to swim off her frustration.

"Teach me to swim," Bekka said after she watched Aubrey do laps. She spent the rest of the afternoon turning into a prune, but she managed to swim the length of the pool.

Dad grilled burgers and they ate outside in the cool of the evening. Bekka wore jeans and her purple shirt.

"Take my picture." She thrust her phone at Aubrey, the phone she'd found lying on the bed when she lifted her backpack. She had not apologized about her accusations. "I have to show the guys at work I'm wearing it, or they won't believe me."

After dinner they watched a movie. Bekka loved Mom's favorite chick flick, *You've Got Mail*.

"It's a remake of an old movie." Mom pulled out her DVD of *The Shop Around the Corner* with Jimmy Stewart in the Tom Hanks role.

When the second film finished, Bekka was clearly deep in thought. "Both are about falling in love with someone you haven't met. You know them through letters and through e-mail. The feelings are the same in both movies. It's only the way they're expressed that's changed."

Mom nodded encouragingly. It was clear Bekka had a point to make.

"You're going to church tomorrow, right? And my family's going to church tomorrow. It's faith for both families. It's only the way it's expressed that's different." She rose. "I need to think about that some more, but first I need to sleep. Swimming wears you out."

Aubrey led the way upstairs. She was spending the night in her old bedroom while Bekka had Scott's old room.

"Where's Scott?" Bekka asked as she dropped onto his bed.

"He has his own apartment. It's nearer his job. We'll see him and Maddie tomorrow at church."

"Why aren't we staying at your apartment?"

"Here you have not only your own bed but your own bedroom."

"I've never had my own bedroom."

"Well now you can find out how you feel about it."

The next morning, Bekka grew wide-eyed the moment she walked into church. Men and women sat together. The music was up tempo, especially to someone used to the slow hymns of the *Ausbund* with the chantlike unison singing. Some people clapped to the music. Some raised their hands. Many read Scripture from their own Bibles, while others followed the words projected on a large screen. The pastor was a great storyteller and made people laugh with a tale from his boyhood, but his message was solid.

"Wow!" Bekka leaned back in her seat as they drove back to Aubrey's parents for dinner. "That was fun!"

Aubrey laughed. "Glad you liked it."

At the dinner table Bekka waited until dessert to question Mom.

"Okay, Aunt Abbie, why did you leave?" Bekka leaned forward in her chair, her body language showing her intensity. "For some reason they still like you even though you left. If I leave, I'll just tell them the same thing you did so they still like me."

Mom set her coffee cup back on its saucer. "Bekka, you can only give them my reasons if they are honestly your reasons too. You may not lie about something so important."

"I wouldn't lie," Bekka protested.

Mom leveled her most piercing gaze on the girl. "I think you're lying to them now."

"No I'm not. They know I'm here."

"I don't mean this precise moment. I mean now in general. Like with your boyfriend."

Bekka shot Aubrey a dirty look. Aubrey shrugged. She'd done the right thing in telling her mom, no matter how Bekka felt about it.

"And like with your phone. What will you tell them about where it comes from if they find it?"

"They won't know how much it costs. I'll just say . . ." Her voice trailed off when Aubrey's mom raised an eyebrow. "Oh."

"Deceit is a slippery slope, Bekka. If you decide to leave, you could just cut and run. Many do. In the short run it's easier. But I'm glad I did it my way."

"Tell me your story, Aunt Abbie. I know what my mom and the aunts say, but I never heard you tell it."

Mom studied her for a moment before she spoke. Aubrey thought she was waiting to gauge if Bekka was finally going to hear what she said.

"Please?" Bekka asked.

"I left for reasons of faith."

Bekka frowned. "What does that mean? You didn't believe in Gott anymore?"

"I came to believe in God differently. I came to believe in salvation by grace, not works."

Bekka stared without comprehension. "I don't get it."

"It means salvation is a free gift from God, given because He loves us. It's not something we earn."

Bekka still frowned in confusion.

Mom smiled briefly, then grew serious. "What you need to know about me, Bekka, is that I didn't leave because I wanted more freedom. I didn't leave because I wanted a better education. Both are sound reasons for many who leave, but for me the issue was salvation by works or by grace. I chose grace because I think that's what the Bible teaches, and I've never regretted it."

"They say you left for Uncle Turner." Bekka glanced at her uncle at the head of the table.

Mom smiled. "I didn't meet Turner until more than three years after I left. I'd been living with some girlfriends, working and taking night courses. I met him at church when he moved to the area for a new job. I married him five years after I left. He was a wonderful bonus in my new life"—Mom sent him a warm smile, which he returned—"but he was not the reason I chose it. Think carefully before you decide, Bekka."

Aubrey drove Bekka, dressed in her Amish garb, home in the early evening.

"I had a wonderful time. I really did," Bekka said as they turned into the family's farm lane. "Can we do it again?"

"Probably." Aubrey felt delighted the weekend had gone so well and relief that it was moments from being over.

Bekka gave her a sly smile. "Maybe Carter can come next time?"

Aubrey raised an eyebrow at her.

"Hey." Bekka grinned. "You gotta ask." She picked up her backpack. "I loved swimming and the movies. Even church was fun. I don't have the vaguest idea what your mom was talking about with that grace or works thing, but she is a nice lady who makes a great roast."

Aunt Susie appeared on the porch and Aubrey waved. "Your mom's a nice lady too, Bek. Be kind to her, okay? She's worried about you."

Bekka opened the door. "I know. I'm a millstone about her neck."

"Try to be a polite millstone, okay?"

With a hoot of laughter Bekka climbed from the car.

14

Sally was glad when Sunday morning arrived. She needed to go to church. She needed to be with her people, to see her family and friends.

Not that she could tell any of them about the turmoil inside. They wouldn't understand. They'd say, "How can you even think of an Englisher?" And she'd answer, "I don't know. I didn't plan it." She had no idea why she was attracted to him. But she recognized that she was skating close to disaster.

She was the oldest of ten, with four brothers and five sisters, and she'd watched over babies her whole life. Watching over Miriam's little ones was as natural as getting up in the morning and falling asleep at night. She loved her life—her *Amish* life—and she looked forward to having her own husband, her own Bobbeli, her own home to care for.

"You are ready to be a wife," her mother had told her two years ago. "You have only to decide which man will be your husband and the father of your children. Choose carefully. Marriage is forever."

So she had searched for a man she could respect as her mother respected her father. She wanted a man who was kind to her like Daed was to Mamm. She thought they loved each other, but she wasn't sure. They weren't demonstrative. She didn't think she'd ever seen them kiss or even hold hands. But they sought each other's opinions and were considerate of each other. Daed was the head of the house as he should be, but he was never cruel about it.

She watched the Englisher tourists who came to the area on their honeymoons or for vacations. They held hands and walked close, even stopped for a kiss or two right there on the street. She knew such behavior wasn't endorsed by her community, and she certainly didn't want the casual intimacy she'd seen on the TVs of the English women she used to clean for.

What she liked was the *idea* of romance. She liked dreaming of a special man who loved her. It was probably foolish to yearn for such a thing. She'd known that from the time the idea took root. Now she knew it was also dangerous.

After a cold breakfast of foods prepared the day before, she helped Miriam dress the children, then slipped into her light-blue dress, which matched the color of her eyes. She knew it was prideful to be so pleased with her appearance each church Sunday, but she couldn't help it. She prayed for forgiveness and humility as she pinned on her starched white organdy apron with its bib. Lastly she pinned on her Kapp, the narrow satin ribbons falling down her back. If it weren't for the circles under her eyes from sleepless nights, she'd match all the other single girls at service.

Dan Zook would try to talk to her afterward. So would Amos Zook, Dan's cousin. Not long ago she'd been thrilled at the attention of two such fine men. Then the Englisher came to the farm.

She would not think about him. She would not. It was wrong. She brushed a nonexistent wrinkle from her apron and left her room. She went downstairs to find everyone ready to leave.

"Come, Anna." She held out her hand. "We will walk together."

The child skipped over. It amazed the quiet Sally how exuberant Anna always was. She glanced over at Harper, standing by her mother. That one also seemed to brim over with joy.

Anna bounced on her toes. "I'm going to see my cousins."

"You are. And I'm going to see my family."

"But I must sit still in church. Mamm says."

"She's right. Church is where we meet Gott."

It would be nice to see her parents and siblings. They would remind her of who she was without saying a word. In their presence she would be the good daughter and caring sister. She would be one of Gott's people, one of those who obeyed and did so with a glad heart.

The heart that should have been glad felt heavy these days. She sighed. *Gott, I need Your help.*

The little boys in their black trousers, white shirts, and black Sunday vests followed Mahlon out to the porch, slapping on their straw hats as they left the house. Even Joseph wore a hat and vest.

Miriam and the little girls wore black dresses. Miriam wore black stockings and shoes. Everyone's hair was knotted neatly, but only Miriam wore a Kapp. Baby Naomi was nestled in the crook of Miriam's good arm.

Sally studied Miriam. Her face was pale, and her brows were furrowed. She must be suffering from another of the headaches from the concussion. Sally would catch her blinking as she tried to clear her vision, especially in the evening when she was tired. She hoped Aubrey was right—that these symptoms were temporary aftereffects of the accident. It was awful to see someone as sweet and good as Miriam suffer.

Aaron brought the buggy to the house so Mahlon could climb in without having to walk to the barn. Aaron helped Miriam in, then handed up Harper and Joseph, who squeezed between their parents. Naomi sat on Miriam's lap.

"Come on, boys," Aaron called to Asa and Ben. He held little Mahlon's hand. "Let's see if we can walk fast enough to beat your parents."

Sally and Anna walked behind the boys and watched Aaron remind them to stay to the side of the road. Automobiles rounded the curves unexpectedly, and one misstep could put a child in their path.

She had to admit Aaron was good with the children. He was a good man and certainly did a better job for Mahlon than Jake had ever done. He was handsome and tall, smart and polite, but she felt no spark when she saw him. Life would be a lot simpler if she felt for him what she felt for his English friend.

What is wrong with me?

Still she was glad he showed no particular interest in her beyond that of a friend. It would be awkward if he did since they were both living at the Eabys' and eating at the same dinner table. She would not want to feel so awkward that she had to leave before her job was finished.

But it was Trent who made her heart trip.

Yesterday had been amazing. When she'd found him on his knees giving Anna and Harper lessons in weeding, she was overcome. She was sure she had actually felt her heart melting. How many men would care about children and weeds?

Then he'd driven them to the nursery in his fancy car. It was a beautiful vehicle, comfortable and fast, but it was a car, a symbol of all the things she wasn't and never would be. She'd ridden in taxi vans many times without any hesitation, but this was different.

She shouldn't have gone. She'd hesitated before saying yes, knowing she should say no, but he'd gazed at her with such hope. He wanted her to ride with him as much as she wanted to go.

She sighed. It wasn't like they could fall in love and he'd become Amish for her. No one became Amish. Well, hardly anyone. You had to be born Amish and grow up Amish to understand what being Amish was. It wasn't just giving up cars and electricity. They were merely outer trappings. Being Amish was a way of thinking. It was a pattern of belief. It was not "finding yourself," like the English said. It was losing oneself to the community and to Gott.

As she walked down the road holding Anna's hand, she had to

smile as she studied Aaron's back. His vest was too small for him. It was past time for his mother to make him a new one. Or maybe they didn't wear vests in Iowa and he was wearing a borrowed one. She had no way of knowing.

They followed the buggies pulling into Ammon Stoltzfus's drive and watched all the families climb out. Aaron went to join the young men releasing the horses from the buggies and tethering them to the large circular feeding trough. The buggies were lined up in neat rows in the side yard. Ammon worked in construction and didn't have a farm or a large property. Careful use of space was important.

Sally and Anna walked into the house, where the women gathered. The men congregated in the backyard, and Sally was pleased to see someone had been thoughtful enough to get Mahlon a chair. When it was time for the service to begin, the men would line up by age and enter the room where the benches were lined up and waiting. Married men went first, then single men and boys followed. Married women with small children came next. The single women entered last and sat at the back on the women's side.

From her seat on the end of a row, Sally could see both Dan and Amos, her would-be suitors. They had sober expressions appropriate for worship, but she was aware that they glanced over at her more than once. She ignored them. Her sister Rhoda in her Sunday best sat beside Sally and poked her in the side when Dan tried to catch her eye. She ignored Rhoda too.

She was surprised to see Jake sitting with the single men. She was not surprised to see the glares of dislike he shot at Aaron and Mahlon. He even glared at her as if his problems were her fault. She shivered as if someone had slipped ice cubes down her back.

The service began with the singing of one of the lovely old songs from the Ausbund. Then they sang "Das Loblied," the second hymn sung in every Amish congregation across America. When she first learned this fact, Sally had felt her heart swell as it swelled again today. All her people with all their differences and similarities had this commonality. It held them together. As she sang the rise and fall of the notes, it sewed her heart anew to the community.

Trent could never join this community, and she knew she would never leave. As she bowed her head for prayer, she vowed her allegiance to Gott and to this ordained way of life.

The English man was wonderful but impossible.

Not only was she sad because her feelings for him were wrong. Deep in her heart she feared any other man she married would be second choice. Dan, Amos, anyone else—how could they make her feel the same rush of excitement and warmth Trent did? The same flutter in the stomach? The delicious ache of being more alive in his presence?

A tear slid down her cheek, and she felt Rhoda's questioning gaze. She was making a sacrifice to please Gott, just as Jesus had when He died on the cross. She squeezed her eyes tight. *I choose You, Gott. I choose Your people. My people.*

15

When Aubrey finished her session with Miriam and Mahlon on Monday, she found Aaron and Trent talking by Trent's shiny black convertible, its top down.

She joined the men. "So how's Peaceable? Is he okay? And did you find Tom? Was he all right?"

Aaron cocked an eyebrow at her. "Full of questions today, aren't you?"

Aubrey flushed. She probably did sound a bit hyper. "Here's another. Do you know anybody who will answer me?"

Trent laughed. "I think she got you, buddy."

"A shot through the heart." Aaron put his hand to his chest.

She fake-glared at him, then laughed. He was so much fun to spar with.

"Let me answer the questions in order." He ticked them off on his fingers. "One—Peaceable is as crotchety as ever, maybe more so since Jake mistreated him, but I'm confident he'll come around in time. Two—he's physically recovered from the whipping. Three—we did not find Tom. Consequently I can't answer question four, but I don't think things look good for him. And five—I think I answered you."

"You did. Thank you." She sighed. "That's about what I expected. Poor Tom."

"Don't waste too much time mourning him, Aubrey." Trent smiled at her. "He's probably fulfilled his purpose. Chances are he was a delicious dinner for another family who probably had no idea where he came from."

"Like I said, poor Tom." He'd strutted around the animal enclosure so proudly, his tail spread as if he knew he was a pretty boy. Now all those beautiful feathers might make someone's duvet extra warm on cold winter nights. And Tom himself—it didn't bear dwelling on. That was what came of thinking of animals as pets.

"I think you're right, Trent." Mahlon moved smoothly across the drive on his crutches. "The bird is gone forever. And I think we all know who took him. He's a loss, though not that much of one, at least financially. But it is another sin to add to the tally Jake needs to confess."

Before the congregation? Aubrey thought that was what Mahlon meant. Did anybody actually have the nerve to stand in front of all their family and friends and admit they were wrong about something? She wasn't sure she'd ever have the courage. Would they want her to confess her stupidity with Ethan? But that wasn't sin. That was just idiocy. Of course it had been a sin on Ethan's part, but she couldn't see him confessing before anyone, congregation or cops—if they ever found him.

And thinking of Ethan, she couldn't stop a smile.

"Have you found some bit of humor in all this that we haven't?" Aaron asked curiously. He and Trent were watching her, confusion on both faces. They were, after all, talking about holding someone accountable for a wrong, and she was standing there smiling.

She shook her head, but inside she was celebrating that for several days she hadn't thought about Ethan as anything other than a thorn in her side, and she certainly didn't miss him. Her broken heart might finally be healed.

She glanced at Aaron, the man she could not get involved with, and knew he was why Ethan had slipped to the edges of her mind. Now Ethan was just a thief who'd taken advantage of her, not a man whose false affection she'd mourn forever. So he hadn't been the man she'd thought he was. His loss. She'd moved on.

She felt her smile building again, but before it burst out, the front door of the house opened, capturing her attention. Sally came onto the porch, followed by Harper and Anna. When Sally caught sight of Trent, a smile wreathed her face for an instant before she wiped her expression clean.

Harper pushed her way past Sally when she caught sight of her father. "Daed! Daed!"

"No, Harper!" Sally grabbed for her and caught her before she tried the steps again. She took the little girl firmly by the hand and helped her down. As soon as her feet hit the ground, Harper pulled free of Sally's hand and raced to her father. She held her arms up.

He smiled and indicated his crutches. He then reached out and patted her head.

Harper pouted. Daed was supposed to pick her up.

Before Aubrey could think of a way to redirect the child, Anna ran up to her little sister. "You want to visit Missy, Harper?"

"Missy!" Harper's sad face became one huge smile. She took Anna's hand and together they ran to the barn.

When the little girls came out of the barn, Anna was holding the small brown hen and Harper was jumping with excitement beside her. They sat under a tree, and Anna passed the hen to Harper who ran her hand gently down Missy's back. The hen leaned into her, eyes closed as she enjoyed the affection.

Sally aimed a shy smile at Aubrey, studiously ignoring Trent. "May I talk to you a minute?"

"Sure." Aubrey moved away from the men and Sally followed.

"I'm concerned about Miriam." Sally glanced toward the house. "She is having such bad headaches."

Aubrey leaned against her car. "I can't talk about one of my patients, Sally. It isn't allowed."

"I know that. I just thought maybe you could pass the word to her doctor or something."

"It hasn't been long since the accident. I think time will take care of the headaches. The brain is like a loose ball in the skull, and Miriam's got shaken badly, knocking against the hard bone. It needs time to heal."

"If you're sure. I wanted you to know, since she might not tell you."

"Thank you. I will watch her and make sure to pass it along to her physician. I'm glad you told me, Sally."

Sally nodded, satisfied. Her gaze lingered on Trent before dropping to the ground. "Excuse me." She rushed away, her cheeks scarlet.

Aubrey watched Sally hurry to the garden and noticed that Trent followed her with his eyes. The girl's blush and Trent's obvious interest told their own story. She saw she wasn't the only one who noticed the sparks between those two. Mahlon glanced from Trent to Sally, an expression of concern washing over his face. *Oh boy. Trouble ahead.* But then Mahlon shrugged, and Aubrey guessed he had decided to worry about that issue some other time. She breathed a sigh of relief.

Aubrey wandered back to the men in time to hear Aaron say, "Um, Trent?"

Trent blinked and came back to the current conversation. "Yes?"

"You brought what I asked you to bring?"

"I did. Let me get it." He hurried to the back of his car, Aaron right behind him. He popped the trunk.

Aubrey glanced at the garden and mentally shook her head. Sally was watching Trent even as she pretended to pick lettuce and peas. Well, not really pretended. She had a couple of heads of lettuce in her container. Aubrey saw Mahlon eyeing Sally too.

If only the girl would be discreet about her interest, but she was so open that such a thought probably never occurred to her. There was an innocence about Sally that came with some Amish girls. They were so protected from the world that they had no guile. They seemed ripe for the picking. She thought of herself, falling into Ethan's clutches. Was Sally Little Red Riding Hood to Trent's Big Bad Wolf?

Not that Trent was a bad guy. He certainly wasn't another Ethan. He was pleasant, polite, and maybe a bit unpolished for a man who drove such a car. But he was genuinely nice. He'd make someone a good catch.

But not Sally. She was Amish to the bone. Pleasantness and politeness wouldn't be enough. Even love wouldn't be enough. She showed none of the interest in the outer world that Bekka did. She was happy in her community, easily accepting its restrictions and benefits. Getting involved with Trent would cause her nothing but turmoil and heartache.

What if she decided to be bold and left her people for him? Not that she ever would, but what if she did? Aubrey was sure the girl wouldn't know how to adjust to living in the outside world. It would be like moving to a foreign land without knowing the language or the customs or the faith practices. Few could manage that well, and Sally was probably not one of the few. She'd be lost without her family, her people, her church.

Aubrey studied Trent in his knit shirt and jeans. There was no way an English man would consider becoming Amish even for the woman he loved. It wasn't a matter of giving up modern conveniences and automobiles. It wasn't a matter of trying to please someone he prized by joining in her life. The issue was a pattern of thought that needed to be taught from birth. Good old American independence and the concept of self-fulfillment—things Trent would have been taught both overtly and covertly his whole life—ran contrary to the Amish way. They were taught to give up their sense of self so as to focus wholly on using their skills to worship Gott and benefit the community.

The Amish had no easy way by which someone could become part of them. They were not evangelistic—they did not seek converts or new members. With very few exceptions, one had to be born Amish to be Amish. Closed circle, closed community.

Aubrey became aware of Aaron waving his hand in front of her face. "Where have you gone?"

She felt herself flush. "Sorry. Daydreaming."

Now Aaron. She'd bet he could leave the community and survive well. There was a sturdiness about him, an assurance. After all, he'd come from Iowa on his own, from one of the most conservative communities in the country, and he was doing well here in a more progressive community. She took a deep breath. There was nothing but danger in such speculation. It might just be wishful thinking on her part. She certainly would never ask anyone to make such a major life-altering decision.

But if he made it himself?

Stop it! Don't go there.

Aaron held an English saddle. He saw her questioning expression and explained, "I've got a theory about our boy Peaceable, and I'm going to test it. Want to see if I'm right?"

"I most certainly do," she said, relieved. Whatever this test was, it would take her mind off her impossible situation with Aaron.

He transferred his attention to Mahlon. "I hope you don't mind, but I'm going to try something. It won't hurt Peaceable at all, and it might make a huge difference."

Mahlon eyed the saddle with curiosity. "As things are now, that horse is a total loss. Anything that might reverse the situation is okay with me."

Trent grabbed a pad from his trunk, the kind that went under a saddle, then closed the trunk.

Aaron entered the barn with Aubrey, Trent, and Mahlon following. Aaron took the pad from Trent. He picked up a halter and lead. By the time they all followed him to the pasture, Aubrey suspected what Aaron's plan was. But would it work?

Her attention was caught by a black horse with one white sock. "You got a new horse."

"We sure did. She's a beautiful animal." Mahlon studied her. The mare raised her head with mild curiosity as did Starry Night and Meltdown, but when they saw there were no carrots or apples coming, they went back to grazing.

"Her name's Maisie." Aaron opened the gate and entered the pasture. "Very sweet disposition. She's a pleasure to work with, unlike someone we know."

He crossed the pasture to Peaceable, who glanced at him, then turned his back as if pretending he wasn't there. Aaron approached him carefully at his shoulder. He made sure the horse saw him coming closer and closer.

When he could no longer pretend he would be left alone, Peaceable watched Aaron approach with an unhappy flick of his tail.

Aaron hooked the halter and saddle over a fence post and came to Peaceable with one hand raised for protection in case the cranky horse decided to try to knock him over. In his other hand he held the saddle pad. When Peaceable didn't protest his presence, he ran his hand down the horse's neck and smoothly slipped the pad onto his back. He grabbed the saddle and placed it on Peaceable, loosely fastening the girth.

Peaceable froze for a few seconds, long enough for Aaron to retrieve the halter and lead and slip them over the horse's head.

"Come on, boy." Aaron started walking, lead in hand. "Let's go."

Peaceable walked at Aaron's shoulder without protest. There was actually a spring in the horse's step and a twinkle in his eye. The lead between Aaron and Peaceable drooped, showing no coercion on Aaron's part or reluctance on Peaceable's.

"Will you look at that!" Trent was impressed as was Aubrey.

Ben and Asa came running to watch the next episode in the saga of Peaceable.

"What are you doing with him?" Asa asked.

Aaron grinned. "Do you have things you like to do more than others? Things you're comfortable with?"

"Sure. I like when Daed lets me help with the horses," Asa said.

"I like when we have the afternoon free to play," Ben added.

"And you have things you don't like?" Aaron asked.

"Weeding the garden." Ben made a face.

"Arithmetic," Asa said with evident misery.

"Well, Peaceable likes some things better than others too." Aaron walked through the gate and into the barn, Peaceable beside him.

Ben frowned. "He likes saddles?"

Aaron laughed. "He likes what they are part of, what he's been trained to do. Get the gate, Asa."

The boy ran to close it. The other horses grazed on, uninterested.

Aubrey followed the parade into the barn, thinking about the foul temper Peaceable had shown again and again. If she didn't know better, she'd think she was watching a different horse.

Aaron dropped the lead and Peaceable stood, waiting. Even when the little girls stood in the big door and Missy gave an indignant squawk at the sight of the horse, Peaceable stood quietly.

Aaron tightened the girth. Then he stepped away from the horse, letting him get used to the saddle.

"Feel familiar, boy?" He stood by Peaceable's head so the horse could see him. "You know your job, don't you? And it's not pulling buggies, is it?"

Peaceable's ears flicked forward as he listened to the soft cadence of Aaron's words. As they all watched, the horse cocked his back leg, a move even Aubrey recognized as a sure sign he was relaxed.

Aaron smiled at his audience as he stroked Peaceable. "I got thinking. You told me, Mahlon, that you bought Peaceable with no knowledge of his background, just a good feeling about him based on his appearance and demeanor. He's gelded, so he's no good for stud. You thought to make him a buggy horse. We tried, but he wanted no part of it. What we didn't know was that Peaceable thinks of himself as a saddle horse. He doesn't want to pull anything down the road, and he's not going to if he has anything to say about it."

He led the horse out of the barn to the large open area at the head of the lane. He gave the horse a final pat and moved down his side. Peaceable turned his head to watch but gave no sign of distress or distrust. Aaron put his foot in the stirrup and swung into the saddle.

Aubrey could have sworn she heard the horse sigh in contentment. It occurred to her that she had never seen Amish people riding their horses, but that didn't mean none did.

Here, horses were for pulling buggies or farm equipment like plows, not riding. Did other Amish communities in other parts of the country ride their horses? Did they ride in Iowa? Was that why the idea had come to Aaron?

"I think Peaceable needs to go to a riding stable," she said.

"I agree," Aaron said.

"I'd never have thought that the saddle was the solution." Trent seemed bothered by the realization. "And I know horses. I grew up with them."

Mahlon's eyes were narrowed in thought, and Aubrey bet he now put Peaceable in the financial plus column.

Aaron was again proving his worth. Which only made Aubrey regret more that she and this fine man could never be more than friends.

16

Aaron sat astride Peaceable and sensed the horse's happiness. He grinned at the upturned faces watching him. "I think for the first time in a long time he's comfortable with what's going on around him. It's what he knows."

Aaron tapped Peaceable's sides with his heels, and the horse began to move. His ears were alert and his eyes bright. He walked past Missy without snorting, and the little hen watched him as if she understood things had changed somehow.

"You're riding like a cowboy!" Asa ran beside them. "Just like in the book I read."

"I'd better go lasso me a bucking bronco, eh? Yeehaw!"

The boy laughed.

Aaron rode to a field behind the house that had been left fallow for the year. It was bright yellow with wild mustard.

Peaceable began to trot and pulled at the reins, wanting to go faster.

"Easy, boy. Let's check the ground. We don't want you stepping into a rabbit hole and breaking your leg."

Aaron held him to a trot as they circled the field. "Okay, Peaceable. It looks safe."

The horse broke into a canter, and his delight at the speed was obvious. When Aaron gave him his head, he flew, mane and tail streaming. In that amazing communication that existed between rider and horse, Aaron felt his pleasure. When his straw hat blew off, he imagined his own hair flying.

When they slowed to a trot, then a walk, Aaron directed the horse back to the yard. He brought Peaceable to the barn, talking to him the whole way. "Good boy. Smart boy." He leaned forward and patted the horse's neck. Peaceable was covered with sweat and joy.

Trent met them at the barn door. "How did you ever come up with this idea? It was brilliant."

Aaron laughed, feeling as energized as the horse. "I got thinking that horses are smart and have preferences like people. Some like to eat peppermints, some don't. Some like getting washed, some don't. Some like pulling things behind them, some don't. They also have different personalities. Maisie and Starry Night are sweet-natured and easygoing. Some can be stubborn and uncooperative if they aren't happy."

Aaron slipped from the saddle and walked Peaceable into the barn. He unfastened the girth and lifted the saddle, resting it on a stall half door. "There we were, trying to make a stubborn horse do something he didn't want to do. And then I started to wonder: What if there was something he liked?"

Aubrey studied the horse, who had his ears perked up and his tail held high. "You've made him a happy boy."

Aaron began to groom Peaceable, who again cocked his left hind leg in an attitude of relaxation. It was the best he'd ever behaved since Aaron had known him.

"I'll check riding stables as his potential home tomorrow." Mahlon started for the door, then stopped. "I'm grateful, Aaron. Denke."

Aaron grinned over Peaceable's back. "My pleasure."

Mahlon hesitated, then cleared his throat. "I'm going to ask you something, and I want you to feel free to say no."

Aaron paused. "Ask away. If I can help, I'll be glad to."

"I'm also asking Aubrey and Trent if they want to be involved. Miriam says I should talk to you all, but I am already so indebted to you all that I'm hesitant."

"So ask." Aubrey glanced at Trent, who nodded. "We'll help too if we can."

Aaron had to smile at her quick answer. She was a woman who liked to come to the aid of those in need. Look at the profession she'd chosen. She was all about making people better. That was one of the many things he liked about her.

"Miriam and I thought we might be well enough to do the things we promised, but we aren't. Her headaches are still bad, and my leg is not healed." He sighed. "The big auction to benefit the Clinic for Special Children in Strasburg is Saturday."

Aaron knew that marriages within a relatively small population had resulted in numerous genetic issues among the Amish, but he hadn't been aware of the home. It shouldn't have surprised him that it existed, though. If ever a people took care of their own, it was the Amish.

Mahlon continued, "Since I'm a member of the local fire company, I was supposed to direct traffic, but I can't. You need two legs and two arms for that job."

"I can do that." Aaron didn't hesitate. How hard could it be to direct a bunch of buggies to park? He'd helped on Sunday, and it hadn't been difficult. If anything, it had been fun.

Mahlon's relief was clear. "I've got a safety vest you can wear."

Aaron tried to imagine how Mahlon, back on this country road with just his horses, got to a fire in time to do any good.

Aubrey voiced his question. "I'm sorry to ask, and I don't mean to be rude, but how do you get to a fire in time from here?"

"My English neighbor down the road picks me up on his way. He is a good man."

"There are both Amish and Englishers in your fire company?" Aubrey asked.

"When someone's home and family are in danger, differences of faith do not matter. All that matters is saving as many lives as possible."

"That's wonderful," Aubrey said quietly.

Aaron had to agree with her.

Mahlon continued. "I've also borrowed several orange cones. Those will help you direct traffic safely."

"Sounds good."

"Most of the attendees will be Amish. We don't advertise like most mud auctions do."

"Mud auctions?" Aubrey asked.

Mahlon grinned. "Held in the spring to benefit fire departments or other worthy causes. It's a muddy time of the year but before farmwork takes up most of our time."

"So it's mostly buggies and horses I'll be dealing with?" Aaron asked.

"Right. I have several teenage boys who will guide people as to where to park and help with the horses. But I can't put someone quite that young in the middle of Route 340 to direct traffic."

The middle of a major road? This might be more than he'd imagined.

"Miriam has goods she's prepared for the auction. They need to be delivered to the auction tent. And she was going to work in the food tent at the table that makes smoothies. Sally will help with the smoothies, but—"

"I can take Miriam's things," Aubrey said. "I'll load the car Friday after work."

Mahlon gave her a grateful smile. "One last thing." He turned to Trent. "I usually set up the electrical connections for the food tent. Can you do that for me?"

Trent swallowed and glanced at Aaron, who nodded reassuringly. "Sure. I'll be glad to help."

"Wonderful. Denke," Mahlon replied. "I'll go and tell Miriam she was right. We are blessed to have such generous people in our lives." He continued to the door, shooing the little girls before him. "Let Missy go, Harper. It's time to go check on your mother."

Anna took Missy from Harper and set her on the ground. She and Harper followed their father to the house. Missy fluttered up to her favorite spot in the haymow.

Sally walked into the barn. Once her eyes got used to the dimness, she glanced around for Trent. She found him, but she couldn't meet his gaze. Aaron met Aubrey's gaze and rolled his eyes. She covered her mouth with a hand to stop a giggle.

"Did Mahlon ask you all to help with the auction?" Sally asked the ground.

"He did," Aaron said. "We all agreed."

She glanced up at Trent. "All?"

"All."

Her smile was brilliant. When she wasn't busy being shy, she was a pretty girl. And Trent obviously thought so too. He walked to her and spoke softly. Aaron couldn't hear what he said, but the two of them walked out of the barn together.

"Oh boy." Aubrey hurried to the door. "They're walking to the field you rode around."

Aaron ran the body brush over Peaceable, making his coat gleam. "Give Trent points for thinking of that. Private because of distance, but visible for propriety's sake."

He clipped the lead to Peaceable. "Wait while I put him to pasture, and we can follow them. I have to go find my hat, which is out there somewhere."

As they walked several yards behind Trent and Sally, Aaron couldn't help but be amused by the picture they all made: two cross-cultural couples with complications galore.

He turned his attention to the woman beside him. "So I want to hear the rest of the Ethan story. You broke up and he left you heartbroken."

Aubrey shook her head. "He left me broke is what he did."

Aaron wasn't sure he understood. "Broke as in your money was gone?"

"Stolen is more like it. That's why I feel like such an idiot. I let a charming guy con me out of $55,000."

Aaron stopped and stared. "That's a lot of money."

"Tell me about it. Most of it was a loan, but the rest was all of my savings. The part that makes me so mad at myself is that I gave it to him. Just handed it over."

He resumed walking. "You're a smart lady. How did that happen?"

"'A fantastic business opportunity,' he said. He was so excited about the potential. Because he knew me and trusted me, he talked his partners into letting me invest. And I fell for it."

"He must have been some talker."

"He was. He made me feel special because he singled me out."

"You *are* special."

"He made it pretty clear that I'm not," she said sadly.

"Well, I think you are."

Her face brightened a little at his words. "The police said guys like Ethan often prey on church people because we want to be trusting and helpful. It's how we're taught to live. Isn't it awful that someone could take advantage of that?"

"It is." He'd never thought about that before, but it made sense. There were all those "one another" verses in the Bible. Love one another. Forgive one another. Serve one another. Be kind to one another. Judge not one another.

"I tell you, Aaron, it makes me doubt my ability to read people. What if someone else tries to con me and I fall for it again? Am I just that gullible? I meet a guy with a smooth line and boom—I get taken again?"

"I doubt it. For one thing, I don't think you'll ever give money to anyone again, especially in that quantity."

"That's for sure."

"For another, you know what to watch for now. Like I said, you're a smart lady."

"But I'm afraid to trust anyone now." It was a whisper. "That's the real thing he took from me. That and my self-confidence."

She was quiet for a few minutes.

He let her think, then spotted his hat. "Be right back." He ran after it and, after brushing it off, put it on. As he rejoined her, he said, "At least you are young and have the time to pay off the loan and be solvent again."

She blinked, clearly taken aback.

He felt like kicking himself. She'd just poured out her heart, and he'd played Mr. Fix-It to a situation that was unfixable. She didn't want solutions. She wanted understanding. "That came out wrong, Aubrey. I don't mean to minimize what you went through."

"Mmm." She walked on, eyes downcast, clearly unhappy.

Up ahead, Trent and Sally seemed to be having a great time. Trent was obviously a better man than he was.

Aaron put a hand on Aubrey's arm. She turned.

"I'm sorry. I'm sorry for what happened to you. I'm sorry for how it makes you feel. I'm sorry I'm so bad at saying the right thing."

She gave him a sad little smile. "And I'm sorry I'm so touchy on this topic."

"Friends?" he asked.

"Friends."

He could breathe again.

17

Sally went hot, then cold when Trent asked her to walk with him. Her stomach fluttered, and she pressed her hand against it to calm it. She should say no. She *must* say no. Just yesterday she'd told Gott she chose Him and her people, and she meant it.

He started toward the field where Aaron had just ridden Peaceable. When she hesitated, he stopped and waited for her. "You can tell me about the auction while we walk."

She took one step in his direction, then another. After all, what harm could a walk around the field do? And he did need to learn about the auction, didn't he?

So she told him. "There are two big white tents—one for the auction, and one for the food." She loved the benefit auction. People came from miles around, people she rarely saw except at large events like this one. "In the auction tent there is Simon Mueller up front talking so fast you can't understand him until he yells, 'Sold!'" She laughed. "When I was little, I would sit for hours just watching him and trying to make out the words. I couldn't believe anyone could talk that fast. Yet somehow things get sold. Apparently other people can understand him just fine."

"Sounds interesting. Is it something like this?" Trent did a great imitation of Simon.

She gaped at him. "How did you know that? You've never met Simon, have you?"

Trent laughed. "No, but I've been to my share of auctions."

His shoulder brushed hers as they walked, and a shiver went down her side. She felt her cheeks grow hot.

"And the food tent!" Maybe if she kept talking, he wouldn't have such an effect on her. "You could spend hours in there going from table to table, having a wonderful time committing the sin of gluttony."

Trent laughed, and she was delighted to get that response from him. Making jokes wasn't a strength of hers, but maybe she should work on it more.

"Tell me about your family," Trent said when she ran out of words about the auction.

She stared at him, surprised. "You don't want to tell me about yours?" Most guys wanted to talk about their lives, not ask about a woman's. Not that they all bragged. They just liked to talk about what was important to them.

"Maybe I'll tell you about mine someday." He gave her a grin that weakened her knees. "Today I want to hear about yours."

Her face warmed with pleasure. "My father is a farmer who grows alfalfa and corn to feed our cows. He likes farming but has a secret wish for rubber tires for his tractor—"

"He has a tractor?" For some reason Trent seemed surprised.

"Oh, not for in the fields. He uses it in the barnyard for powering tools."

"Still, a tractor."

"With big iron wheels. He'd love rubber tires so he can drive quietly down the road, but they aren't allowed. It's a family joke we tease him about."

"And he wouldn't try to sneak them?"

"He wouldn't. First off, he couldn't sneak something that big, and secondly, he would never do anything against the Ordnung. I think the second one is more important to him, actually." She smiled as she thought of her father. "He's always taught us to follow Gott by following the Ordnung. He'd never deliberately disobey."

"He sounds like my father."

"Really?" She glanced up at him. "How?"

Trent had turned an interesting shade of red. "I just mean my father tries to do everything right too. He's a man I respect."

"Like I respect my father." She understood what he meant. "We are blessed to have such men raise us." She grinned. "But mine's always willing to try something different."

"Like?"

"He was the first one in our district to buy one of the wooden swing sets for us kids when we were little. It had two swings and a slide and what we called a castle over the top of the slide." She giggled. "The bishop came to talk to Daed about having something so frivolous. He brought his son with him and left him outside with us. The little boy was crying because his mother had just died, so my siblings and I encouraged him to come and play. When the bishop came outside again, his son was going down the slide, laughing. He hadn't laughed in days. We were allowed to keep the play set, and soon other families had them too."

"That is a wonderful story. You know, I've read about other Amish communities that are much stricter than you seem here."

"How do you mean?"

"No tractors."

"Then certainly no rubber tires." She laughed.

"No indeed. No chain saws. No indoor flushing toilets."

"I'm glad that last one's not us. It must be terrible in the winter." She shivered at the thought.

"You'll get no argument from me," Trent said, laughing.

"You don't have a girl you're courting?" she blurted, then immediately blushed. She should not have asked such a personal question.

He met her gaze, and she thought she saw more than she should in his eyes. "I haven't found anyone I was interested in before."

Her heart jumped with delight and fear. She must change the subject—fast. She grabbed the first thing that came to mind. "Our farm is just down the street and around the corner." She pointed vaguely in the right direction. "You've probably driven past it. There's a big flower garden out front where my mother grows beautiful flowers. She makes them into bouquets and sells them. She has a shelter my father built for her to sell her arrangements. English ladies stop and buy from her all the time. Five dollars a bouquet."

Trent seemed willing to follow her change of topic. "My mother has a wonderful flower garden too. It's huge. I should tell her about your mother's."

"Really? You'd tell her about my Mamm?"

"Why wouldn't I?"

"Well, my mother's Amish and yours is . . ." Her voice trailed off. There were those terrible differences once again.

"A good idea is a good idea. Why shouldn't both of our mothers enjoy flowers?" She flushed with pleasure. Trent watched her as she talked, laughing at the right places, encouraging her. It was a heady feeling to be the center of someone's attention.

She immediately felt conflicted. It was wrong. Prideful. And he was wrong for her. How selfish of her to seek the attention and approval of a man she could not become involved with. The joy she'd felt at his attention turned to despair.

Gott im Himmel, help me!

They had walked the entire circumference of the field and were almost back at the house, and not a moment too soon for her peace of mind.

Trent stopped, and she automatically stopped too.

"Will you go for a ride with me in my car?" His eyes pleaded with her. "Maybe go to dinner?"

She stared at him in something close to horror. He was asking something that she yearned for deep in her heart.

She felt tears building and blinked hard. "I can't," she managed, little above a whisper. She had chosen Gott. "I can't."

And she ran inside.

The crackle of a police radio and the flash of revolving lights on the wall of his room in the barn woke Aaron Tuesday night. He jumped out of bed and looked out the window. Yup. A police car.

What was it doing here? He yanked on pants and a shirt and ran outside to catch whoever it was before they woke the whole house. He managed to intercept a young officer about to climb the front steps.

"Don't wake them!" he hissed. "They're still recovering from a bad accident. I can help you."

"Is this the Eaby farm?" the officer asked.

"It is. What's wrong?" Was it his family? Had something terrible happened? That would be the only reason for the police to be here at this hour.

"Do you have horses?"

What Amish farm didn't? "Yes, several." His heart steadied. Everyone must be safe if he was asking about the horses. "Currently five adults and a colt."

"Are they here?"

"Of course they're here." But his heart began to thud again.

"Are they in the barn?"

"The pasture. You want to check on them?" Aaron started for the barn, the officer following.

"There are some loose horses wandering down the road," he said. "Some guy almost hit one of them, then promptly had a near miss with another."

What a catastrophe that would have been, for both the man and the animals. Aaron led the way out the back of the barn to the pasture. He stopped so suddenly the officer almost ran into him. "They're gone."

The pasture loomed empty, the gate open.

"Looks like someone was careless last evening." The officer was clearly displeased by the situation.

"It was closed firmly. I know it."

The officer, whose name tag read *Milligan*, said nothing, but his skepticism was obvious.

"Mahlon can verify I shut the gate."

Officer Milligan checked his notebook. "Mahlon Eaby? The one recovering from an accident?"

"That's right. He comes out each evening to do a final check on the horses."

"What's going on out here?" came a voice cutting through the night.

Aaron and Officer Milligan turned to find Mahlon, dressed much as Aaron in his hurry, balancing on his crutches in the barn doorway.

"The horses are missing." Aaron gestured to the empty field.

"That's not possible." But possible or not, it was obviously the truth.

Officer Milligan checked his notes, then studied Aaron. "Who are you?"

"The assistant horse trainer. Mahlon, tell him the gate was securely fastened last night."

"It was. We both checked it."

"Then why is one of your horses standing in the middle of the road? Another is at your neighbor's." He checked again. "Alvin Esch."

Mahlon shook his head as if to clear confusion and swayed a little.

Milligan saw it and put out a hand. "Why don't we find you a seat where there's light, Mr. Eaby? I can't do anything out here in the dark. We can talk where you'll be comfortable."

"My room has a chair. We can talk there." Aaron led the way to his room and helped Mahlon into the lone chair, then lit his lantern.

"You said two horses were in the road." Aaron leaned against the doorjamb while Officer Milligan stood in the middle of the room. It wasn't much—just the chair, a bed, a battery-operated lantern for light, a bureau with a pitcher and basin for washing—but it was comfortable and generous of Mahlon and Miriam to provide for him. Several books and a Bible sat on the bureau top.

"Mahlon," a voice called from outside. "I have your horse."

When Mahlon started to rise, Aaron held out his hand. "Let me get him."

Mahlon dropped back into the chair, gray with fatigue.

Aaron left the barn, followed by Officer Milligan, to find Alvin Esch with Meltdown on a tether beside him.

Aaron approached Meltdown and patted the horse's neck. "Hello, old boy. What are you doing out so late? We gave you a curfew."

Meltdown nickered softly and bobbed his head.

"Someone made you do it, huh?"

Meltdown bumped his shoulder, and Aaron laughed. "You want to go back to your nice safe pasture, don't you? In a minute. I need to talk to these men."

"Do you always talk to the horses?" the Amish man asked. His bemused expression said he never did.

"I do. It seems to soothe them."

"Must be the Iowa way."

Aaron shrugged. "It's my way. Thanks for bringing Meltdown back. Is he horse one or horse two?"

"Horse two." Alvin took a deep breath and launched into his story of the night. "Some man bangs on my door, waking the whole house, including the baby, who had just fallen asleep. 'There's a horse in the middle of the road,' he says. He is not a happy man. 'The middle of the road!' he yells. 'Is it yours?' And sure enough, there was a gelding, all wide-eyed and twitchy and scared, in the road in front of my lane. I put him up in my barn and the man drives off, only to be back before I even get from the barn to the house. 'There's another one!' he roars, like it's my fault. 'It made me drive off the road! I'm calling the police,' he says. And he must have."

Officer Milligan nodded. "I got the call at 12:55. Mr. Esch here helped with this horse, the second one. Meltdown, I think you called him. I said I'd drive ahead to check if he could bring the horse here."

"The first horse is still in my barn," Alvin said.

"Thank you, Mr. Esch." Aaron held out his hand.

Alvin shook it with a puzzled expression. "Who are you?"

"Aaron Ropp. I'm helping Mahlon while he recovers from his accident. Mahlon's in my room in the barn if you want to say hello. I'm going to put Meltdown back in the pasture."

A few minutes later Aaron joined the men in his room. Mahlon, his face drawn, sagged in the chair. "Would you mind going with Alvin to get whichever horse is there?"

"Of course. Perhaps Officer Milligan could drive Mr. Esch and me?"

"Sure," the officer replied. "After I drop you two off, I'll drive the length of the road to be certain there are no more horses ready to bring a driver to ruin. If they're in a pasture or if they wandered into a patch of woods, we won't find them until morning."

Mahlon closed his eyes and leaned his head back. "How did this happen?"

"That's a good question," Officer Milligan said. "Its counterpart is, who unlocked the gate, since you're sure the gate was locked?"

Aaron knew who, and he knew Mahlon did as well—which was probably one reason why he was looking so defeated.

"Let's go and let Mr. Eaby get back to bed." Officer Milligan moved to the door. "Sorry for having to disturb you, sir."

"You were just doing your job, and I am grateful for it," Mahlon replied.

Aaron, Alvin, and Officer Milligan filed out.

As they rode the short distance to Alvin's house, they passed a car in a ditch and a tow truck working to remove it.

"The second horse," Officer Milligan said.

"The one I brought to you," Alvin added.

"The first one was in the opposite lane," Officer Milligan explained. "Though it scared Mr. Jensen badly, it didn't cause any harm. Mr. Jensen was nice enough to contact Mr. Esch. It was the second horse—the one now back in your pasture—that did this. It was standing right in his lane as he rounded a curve. He swerved to miss it and ended up in the ditch." Officer Milligan gave a wheeze that might have been misplaced laughter. "Mr. Jensen is not a happy man."

Alvin led Aaron to the barn as Officer Milligan drove away. "This is a nice horse you got here. I'm in the market for another one."

"You'll have to talk with Mahlon about that." They walked into the barn and Peaceable turned toward the noise, then nickered when he recognized Aaron. "But not about this horse, I'm afraid."

"Already spoken for?"

"More or less. He's not suited to farmwork. He's a riding horse through and through."

When Aaron arrived at the farm on Peaceable's back, Mahlon was sitting on the house steps.

Aaron slid to the ground. "Are you all right, Mahlon? I was worried about you in there."

"Physically I'm just tired. My heart is what's sore."

Aaron sat beside him. "Jake?"

"I don't know a lot about the English legal system. How much trouble will he be in?"

"I don't think there's much that would happen unless we could prove Jake released the animals with the intention to hurt someone."

"You mean like he put them in the road so there'd be an accident?"

Aaron nodded. "I'm concerned because English people like to sue. That Mr. Jensen might sue you for the damage to his car and his pain and suffering."

"Sue me?" Mahlon asked, his voice alarmed. "I didn't do anything. I certainly didn't let the horses loose."

Aaron held up a hand. "I shouldn't have said anything. I'm sorry. Please don't worry. Mr. Jensen's insurance should take care of any problems with his car."

The men sat quietly as the sky began to lighten, Peaceable standing peacefully, half-asleep, head low and back leg cocked.

"I know it's wrong," Aaron said quietly, "but I'm finding it hard to turn the other cheek where Jake is concerned. I can't help feeling something needs to be done about him."

Mahlon sighed. "Gott is our judge. One day, Jake's sins will find him out. Until then, it is our job to forgive."

18

When Aubrey arrived at the farm for her appointment with Mahlon and Miriam on Wednesday, she found a police car in the lane.

She climbed out of the car, her heart hammering. Why were the police here? The Amish and the police had a cordial but distant relationship. The Amish preferred to handle their problems their way. Only something serious would account for police presence.

She ran toward the barn. "Aaron? What's going on?"

There was no answer. She ran to the house. As she rushed up the steps, the house door opened and Mahlon and an officer walked out. The men shook hands.

"They're all accounted for, and that's good," the officer was saying. "I'll say again that I'm glad things worked out so well. Someone could have been seriously hurt. As it is, a car was wrecked. This wasn't merely a prank."

"I know. And I truly appreciate what you're saying, but all I have is suspicion. I don't want to blacken a name without proof."

The officer shrugged and went down the steps, tipping his hat to Aubrey as he passed. He climbed into his car and left.

"What's wrong?" Aubrey could stand her ignorance no longer. "Did someone get hurt? One of the children?"

"Nothing like that." Mahlon followed the departing police car with his eyes.

Asa slipped from behind his father. "Someone let the horses out during the night!" he told Aubrey.

Aubrey's breath caught. "Someone what?" Surely she'd heard wrong.

Asa gave her a cockeyed grin, a seven-year-old boy caught up in the excitement. "He let the horses out!"

"Were any of them hurt?" Aubrey asked Mahlon in concern.

"Asa, go pick the rest of the strawberries." Mahlon turned the boy toward the field.

"They weren't hurt," he called over his shoulder as he ran to do as his father said, grin still in evidence.

Mahlon held the screen door open. "Come in, Aubrey, and I'll tell you."

Aubrey followed him. Mahlon took a seat in his recliner, a weary sigh escaping as he lowered himself. Miriam appeared at his side with a glass of lemonade in her good hand.

"Drink." She held it out to him. When he took it, she gave his shoulder a squeeze, then returned to the kitchen.

Joseph tottered over and grabbed his father's pant leg to steady himself. He laid his head on Mahlon's knee. "Da." He patted his father's leg, then sat and began trying to untie Mahlon's work boot.

Aubrey smiled at the ordinary little family vignettes and the support they showed for the weary man in the recliner. She took the chair across from him. "Tell me."

He took a sip of his lemonade. "Someone let the horses out of the pasture where they were spending the night."

"You mean someone left the gate open?" Surely Aaron wouldn't be that forgetful.

"No. The gate was closed. I saw it closed when I went to the barn for a final check for the night. Aaron also confirms that fact. Adelaide and the colt were let out too. Different pasture, different gate."

She closed her eyes briefly against the terrible alternative. "Someone opened both gates on purpose."

"He didn't just open the gate and the horses happened to wander out," Mahlon corrected her. "He herded the horses out."

"They wouldn't have left on their own?"

"Maybe. Maybe not. They wouldn't have wandered as far as they did, especially out into the road."

Aubrey thought of the beautiful little colt with the white blaze. "But none of the horses were . . . hurt?" She couldn't bring herself to say the word *killed*.

"No." Mahlon almost smiled. "It's a miracle, really. They're all dark in color and would have blended with the night."

Aubrey could only imagine the damage an animal the size of a horse could do to a car and its occupants. And it could easily go the other way. She thought of the horse that had been killed in Mahlon and Miriam's accident.

Mahlon put his empty glass on the side table. "A driver coming home from the late shift almost hit one. He came around the curve and there was Peaceable. He went to the Esch place, which was the closest farm, and Alvin rescued the horse. Then the same man almost hit Meltdown, who was also standing in the middle of the road."

"Was the driver hurt?"

"No, he was more angry than anything. He crashed his car when he swerved around Meltdown. Aaron found them all. Starry Night was standing in an alfalfa field establishing a friendship with a pair of horses on the other side of a fence in an adjoining field. Maisie was the last one found. She'd wandered into that section of woods down by the school and gotten caught in some brambles. She was terrified."

"Poor thing. And Adelaide and the colt?"

"In the field of wild mustard."

Anna walked carefully across the room with a glass of lemonade in her hand. She offered it to Aubrey, who took it with a smile. "Denke, Anna." She took a sip. The sweet-tart beverage was wonderfully refreshing.

"I must ask a favor," Mahlon said. "I need to go visit the Stoltzfuses. Can you drive me?"

"Of course." So he thought it was Jake. No surprise. She did too.

She waited in the car while Mahlon went to the door. He disappeared inside and she got out her e-reader and tried to read. After a few minutes, she gave up and laid her head against the rest, unable to concentrate. She kept imagining the difficult conversation going on inside.

A shadow fell across her, and Aubrey raised her head to see a young woman standing at her open window. She had blonde hair and wore a blue dress that matched her bright eyes. She had the kind of face that Aubrey guessed was used to smiling, but today it was troubled.

"I'm Mary, Jake's sister. Would you like to come sit under the tree rather than wait in your car for Mahlon? I think it will be cooler."

"Thank you, Mary." Aubrey climbed from the car and followed Mary to a pair of Adirondack chairs under an oak tree. Aubrey slid back into the chair's embrace. "I always feel I won't be able to climb out of one of these, but they're so comfortable, I don't really care."

Mary laughed in spite of the strain in her face. She leaned her head against the chair's back. "My parents are ashamed of Jake."

Not a surprise, given the situation. "They shouldn't be. I heard everyone talking about what wonderful people they are."

Mary's eyes glistened with tears. "But if you train up a child in the way he should go, he will not depart. He will be good."

Aubrey shook her head. "I'm not a parent, but I don't think it's quite that simple. Many wonderful parents have children who turn to wrong behavior. We all get to choose. If we have good parents who have taught us, it is easier to choose right. You have chosen right. According to what I hear, so have your older brothers. Jake has made his own choice to ignore all the good things your parents taught him."

"We don't expect disobedient children."

Aubrey assumed the use of the plural pronoun *we* meant she was referring to the Amish community. "I don't think any parents do, Amish or English. I think all parents want children they can be proud of." Aubrey heard herself. Given the Amish view of Uffgevva, she should rephrase that last bit. "Maybe 'be proud of' isn't the right phrase. That could indicate the parents think they are smart and wonderful, which is not what I mean. Maybe I should say parents want children they can see loving God and caring for and following their teachings."

"I think that's right," Mary agreed. "Jake is far from Gott, and it grieves them, though they try not to show it. But I know how they feel, and it grieves me to see them hurt."

They sat quietly, and Aubrey enjoyed a slight breeze that fanned the leaves above her and lifted the hair on her forehead.

Mary broke the silence. "We don't know where Jake is."

Aubrey gasped. "He's missing?" That would be another blow to Mary's parents.

"We haven't seen him since our last church service," Mary said miserably. "The bishop came to talk with him when Mahlon reported their attempt to help him had failed. He became so angry he yelled at the bishop." There was disbelief in her voice. No one yelled at the bishop. "He ran from the house and we haven't seen him since."

"I'm so sorry, Mary."

Mary sighed. "Daed says he can't come home until he repents and apologizes. He must be held accountable or he will continue to think he can do whatever he wants."

A hard stance, but perhaps a wise one. She was sure Aunt Edna would approve and probably even gentle Mammi. After all, the Ordnung was in place for a reason.

The front door opened, and Mahlon and an older man with a graying beard walked onto the porch. They shook hands gravely, and Mahlon made his way down the steps.

Aubrey pulled herself from the chair and reached the car in time to open the passenger door. Mahlon slid inside and sat staring straight ahead the whole ride home. When they pulled into the lane, he finally spoke. "Denke, Aubrey. That was not one of my favorite visits with that family, and we have been friends for a long time."

"You're welcome. I'm sorry it was hard."

Just then, two little girls came running from the barn crying.

Mahlon grabbed his crutches. "What's wrong?" He hurried to meet the girls.

"She's gone!" Anna called. "Missy's gone!"

Aaron walked out of the barn behind Anna and Harper. He shook his head at Mahlon. When the girls had started getting upset because Missy didn't come to them, he had searched the barn. There was no little brown hen.

Earlier in the day he had been so busy with the horses, first finding them, then calming them and getting them back in the pasture, that he hadn't noticed Missy wasn't staring down, clucking softly, and pacing the floor of the haymow, as she usually did when Aaron tended the horses.

"My guess is that she was frightened last night when Jake was turning the horses loose," Aaron said. "She ran away to hide."

"Or maybe he—" Aubrey stopped short when she remembered the little ears listening.

"Maybe," Aaron agreed.

"Maybe what?" Anna demanded.

Aaron didn't know what to say.

"Maybe she's in with the other hens?" Aubrey rescued the moment.

Everyone peered into the animal enclosure. The goat stood on a tree stump in the middle of the compound. The sheep rested under the overhanging branches of the maple just on the other side of the fence. The hens moved busily about the area as usual. The miniature ponies cropped hay from the basket slung on the side of the lean-to for them. Missy was nowhere in sight.

"Come on, girls." Mahlon started toward the house. "Let's go tell your mother and Sally the news." He started toward the house, two unhappy girls trailing him.

Aubrey gaped at Aaron in astonishment. "Aren't they even going to try to find her?"

Aaron shrugged. "Mahlon's a farmer, Aubrey. A hen is just a hen to him, not a pet."

"But the girls are heartbroken."

"You Englishers." Aaron started for the barn.

"Well, at least we've got heart," she said sharply.

He turned back to her. She stood by her car, hands on her hips, glaring at him. He bit back a smile, knowing it would just infuriate her. He had to admit he liked her spunk. She cared about Missy and Anna and Harper. That deep concern she felt for a creature as small as Missy and as important as the children showed him her character. She was lovely, intelligent, and a pleasure to talk to, but it was her character that made her special.

He'd met many girls in his time, some even as pretty as Aubrey, but none who engaged him as she did. He needed to talk with her about some serious issues—and soon, before someone got hurt.

"Be right back," he told her. He walked into the barn and beyond. He had to wonder if she'd still be there when he returned, or would her anger have gotten the better of her? When he reached Peaceable, he led him into the barn, where he grabbed the saddle and pad, tightened the cinch, and guided the animal into the yard.

She was standing where he'd left her, her hands still on her hips, her scowl firmly in place. When he emerged with Peaceable, she looked surprised, then pleased.

"Are you going to search for Missy?"

He mounted, then smiled down at her. "Peaceable's hearing is better than mine. So's his sense of smell. If she's anywhere near, he may be able to find her."

She beamed at him. "Thank you."

And he felt like a superhero.

He rode down the lane, peering right and left. Just before he reached the road, he turned. He was surprised to see her climbing into her car.

"I have something I need to talk to you about," he called. "Can you wait?"

She shook her head. "I'm cutting it close with my next client. I really need to go. Next time?"

If he had a car, he could drive to her house tonight. Ah, the inconvenience of being Amish. "Sure. We'll talk another time." His gut clenched, but what choice did he have? Another day or two before he told her wouldn't matter. Probably.

He watched her drive away, then turned his attention to Missy. "Ok, Peaceable. Find your friend."

They walked half a mile in one direction without Peaceable giving a sign of anything unusual. Aaron scanned the edges of the fields where the cornstalks were nowhere near as high as an elephant's eye. The fields of wild mustard could easily hide a creature as tiny as Missy among their yellow blooms.

He pulled Peaceable to a stop and turned back toward the farm. Given Missy's size, it was hard to imagine her getting even this far. Truth be told, he didn't have much hope for her. She was little and vulnerable. All she had to do was cross paths with a fox or a badger or one of any number of small predators, and she'd have no chance.

He retraced his steps and continued in the new direction. Cars passed him, but he and Peaceable ignored them. They were passing another field of corn when Peaceable stopped, his head cocked to the side. Aaron cocked his head too but heard nothing.

Peaceable gave a soft whinny, and now Aaron heard a series of faint clucking sounds. Peaceable whinnied again and the clucking grew louder. Then, out of the thigh-high corn flew a little brown hen, right into Peaceable's nose. He shook his head, and she tumbled to the ground with a squawk.

"Missy!"

Aaron couldn't believe he had found her. Or rather, Peaceable had found her. He'd have ridden right past, never hearing the soft sounds she had been making.

Peaceable lowered his head and gave Missy a soft bump. She gave a hen's version of purring. Aaron leaned over and held out his hand, and she jumped up to meet him. He held her snugly against his chest. She burrowed as close as she could, even trying to climb inside his shirt. He could feel her little heart pounding. He had no idea how fast a chicken's pulse should be normally, but he was amazed her little heart didn't burst through her chest.

Peaceable gave a satisfied snort and turned for home without any direction from Aaron.

As they moved down the road, Aaron thought of Aubrey climbing into her car and driving away. If only he could call her back. He not only wanted to talk to her, he needed to. It amazed him how much she had come to mean to him in such a short time.

He wanted to see her face when he told her about Missy. How foolish was it that he wanted to be a hero to her, even in such a small thing as finding a hen?

More importantly, there were serious things they had to discuss. "Next time," she'd said. Hopefully next time wouldn't be too late. He knew with certainty that his future was on the line.

When he and Peaceable reached the house, he slid from the horse's back, Missy still cradled in his arms. She leaned her head forward and clucked at the horse. Peaceable gave a soft nicker. *Their version of "Thank you" and "You're welcome."*

Aaron went to the front door. He knocked and waited. He couldn't stop smiling as he anticipated Anna's and Harper's reactions to his feathery present.

Sally opened the door. When she saw Missy, a brilliant smile lit her face. "Anna! Harper! Come see!"

The reunion was sweet to watch. When he left to take Peaceable back to the pasture, the girls were seated on the steps, Missy cuddled close.

He slipped from Peaceable's back. "You did a good thing, finding that little bird." He gave the horse a carrot.

Peaceable shook his mane as if to say, "And don't I know it."

19

After watching Aaron ride off to find Missy, Aubrey remembered something and hopped back out of her car. She needed to talk to Sally, even if it made her a little late for her next appointment. She knew she was asking a big favor of someone she didn't know all that well, but she didn't know who else to approach.

Aubrey found Sally comforting two distraught little girls inside the house. "Sally? Can I borrow you for a moment?"

The Amish girl extricated herself and had the girls cling to each other, then followed Aubrey to the porch where they could speak in private. "What can I do for you?"

It was best to jump right in. "I have a cousin named Bekka. She's seventeen. She's smart and opinionated and confused. She's not certain she wants to remain Amish. Would you be willing to talk to her?"

"Me?" Sally asked, alarm on her face. "Why me?"

"She needs to talk to someone who loves being Amish."

"You have family who are Amish, don't you? Why not them?"

"It can't be family. They've been lecturing her and making her angry. Quite frankly, she scares them because she's different. They all think I'm trying to get Bekka to leave. I'm not. I do want her to know she has the option, but I don't want to push her in either direction. I want her to see both sides of her choice."

Sally still seemed unsure.

"I have to tell you she has an English boyfriend who is helping her sneak out on dates."

"I've heard that one before. How old is he?"

"Twenty-one."

Sally shook her head. "And she's seventeen? That's not a good combination."

"I agree. So will you talk to her? Let her know it's not all rules and restrictions?"

Sally took a deep breath. "I will, but it may not help. It's wrong to force someone into our lifestyle. Each person must choose this path for his or her life."

"I know. I just want to be sure she doesn't decide to leave because she's mad over things not worth getting mad about. I don't want her to ruin relationships and hurt people who love her. I know she'd regret it later, and I want to make sure she sees the good parts of her heritage. May I bring her over this evening?"

"Sure. Why not?"

It was seven when Aubrey sat on the ground under the maple tree with Bekka and Sally. Bekka had pouted most of the drive, but she cheered up slightly when they stopped for ice cream for themselves and Sally.

Bekka, never one to be shy, got right to the point. "So you like being Amish. Why?"

"I can't imagine being anything different," Sally said.

"I can."

"That's what I hear." She turned Bekka's question back on her. "Why?"

"So I can breathe."

When Sally simply nodded, Bekka went on. "I don't like to do any of the things Amish women are supposed to do. I don't like the kitchen. I don't like to cook. I don't like to sew. The thought of putting up vegetables gives me hives."

Sally took her feelings in stride. "So marry someone who doesn't mind if you hire a Maud."

Bekka gasped. "Can I do that?"

"Why not?"

"My dad would think it a foolish waste of money."

"But it's your husband, not your father, who has to agree with the Maud. Maybe he'll see it as a charitable act, especially if you hire someone whose family needs her to have an income."

"Oh." It was clearly a new thought to someone who'd always been under her father's authority.

"But if you aren't keeping your home, what will you do with your time?" Sally asked.

"That's easy. I'd read. Learn stuff. Study the universe." Bekka smiled up at the clear blue sky. "There are marvelous things out there, things we can't see with our eyes but that super cameras can take pictures of. And those things are beautiful!"

Sally followed her gaze. "Really?"

Bekka scowled. "And you don't care, do you?"

Sally smiled. "I care about that as much as you care about cooking dinner tonight."

"And that's my problem." Bekka pointed accusingly at Sally. "Every Amish woman I know cares about dinner and none of them care about supernovas."

"Do you think all English women care about supernovas?"

They both turned to Aubrey, who said, "Not me, not really. It's interesting to see pictures every so often, and I'm impressed with the technology that makes those pictures possible, but that's about it. And I personally don't know any astronomers."

Bekka became almost belligerent. "I want a telescope to watch the stars."

Aubrey shrugged. "So save your money."

That piece of logic deepened Bekka's scowl.

Sally leaned forward. "Here's my question, Bekka. Are you strong enough to be different if you remain among your family and friends who love you?"

"And here's mine," Aubrey said. "Are you strong enough to leave behind the family and friends who love you and whom you love just because they make you feel too different?"

"You have me so confused!" Bekka wailed.

Aubrey understood the feeling. Not that she had it about the choice between being Amish or English, but she felt it every time she thought of Aaron. How could she be falling in love with an Amish man? Maybe she was *already* in love, she had to admit to herself. How could she ever find a resolution to the problem of the great yawning canyon between their cultures?

"If you're that confused, Bekka," Sally said, "you're not ready to make such a major decision yet."

"Life is long, Bek." Aubrey took her cousin's hand. "Take your time. You don't have to decide anything today." Neither did she, now that she thought about it.

"But my parents—"

"They can't make you marry. They can't make you get baptized. Here's my suggestion. Wait at least a year. See if you still love astronomy. See if you still like Carter."

Maybe Aubrey should take her own advice. She should wait a year and see how things stood between her and Aaron.

"I know it feels like you have to decide now. But let's say you live to be eighty. That's sixty-three more years to be Amish or English."

She felt a stab in her heart as she thought of the rest of her own life without Aaron in it.

Aubrey gave Bekka's hand a squeeze. "Take the time to get it right."

"I love being Amish, Bekka." Sally's smile was sad around the edges, and Aubrey had a good idea why. "It's cost me because I was tempted by an English man, but I couldn't imagine giving up my friends, my family, and my Gott. I think Aubrey's advice to wait awhile longer before making such a big decision is good advice."

Bekka stood up. "I need to talk to Carter."

Aubrey knew the conversation was over. Bekka probably wasn't going to take their advice, but she knew she had tried.

Now she had to try to get it right in her own life. All she had to do was figure out what the right thing was.

Nothing bad happened Wednesday night or Thursday. Aaron's hope was that Jake had been frightened by the police presence after he spooked the horses and disappeared. But Thursday night he was wakened by a great commotion in the small animal enclosure.

Aaron quickly dressed and raced outside with the high-intensity flashlight he'd borrowed from Trent.

At first all he heard was the goat bleating, the hens squawking, and the miniature horses whinnying. He scanned for a predator of some kind. Had a fox managed to get through the fence and tried to get the hens, waking the rest of the animals in the process? Then he saw a dark shape, definitely human, trying to grab the uncooperative goat. She kicked and butted and squirmed, all the while bellowing to raise the dead.

The tiny horses raced around the enclosure, whinnying. The hens squawked and ran every which way. The sheep backed themselves into the lean-to and *baa*-ed their distress. If it hadn't been for the present threat, Aaron might have laughed at the chaotic picture.

He flicked on the flashlight and trained it on the figure. Startled and momentarily blinded, Jake Stoltzfus froze. He'd managed to grip the goat around the middle. Taking advantage of Jake's distraction, the goat squirmed and bucked with renewed effort. One of her flailing hooves connected with Jake's knee. With a howl he dropped her, and she raced to the lean-to and scaled it. She stood there, bleating and shaking.

"What do you think you're doing, Jake?" Aaron's voice cut through the animals' commotion. He jumped the fence into the compound, just missing a scurrying hen as he landed. "Nice jeans and T-shirt by the way. I take that to mean you're giving up being Amish? Or is it merely Rumspringa?"

"Get away from me!" Jake raced toward the far side of the compound, limping slightly from the goat's kick.

"Don't you dare run!" Aaron tore after him. "Man up, you little thief!"

Just before Jake hurdled the fence, Aaron tackled him. He and Jake went to the ground and Aaron scrambled until he sat on Jake's chest.

"No!" Jake squirmed and flailed and tried to throw Aaron off. Aaron grabbed one arm and was reaching for the other when Jake swung. Lying flat on his back, he wasn't able to get much behind the swing, but Aaron had no desire to be punched in the face. He ducked so that the blow merely glanced off his shoulder.

As he grabbed for Jake's free arm again, a thought flashed through his mind. What would Aubrey think of him wrestling in the dirt? Would she cheer him on? Or would she be horrified, or worse—disappointed? As always it astonished him how much her opinion mattered.

Immediately following those thoughts came one about what he'd do with Jake after he subdued him. Wake Mahlon? Contact Officer Milligan who'd been here the night of the horses? Jake swung again, forcing Aaron to focus completely on the squirming eel beneath him. Winning this fight wasn't a foregone conclusion.

"Stop it! This minute!"

The voice came out of the dark, and Aaron wasn't certain whether the command was for him or Jake. Beneath him, Jake went absolutely still. "Daed?" he asked, disbelief lacing the word.

Aaron took advantage of the stillness and dragged the man to his feet. He kept a grip on Jake's shirt so he couldn't bolt. He also made sure to stand close behind him in case he turned and tried to strike again.

A man materialized out of the darkness holding a battery-powered lantern aloft. Its warm glow illuminated the face of Reuben Stoltzfus. "Jacob, what are you doing?"

Jake ducked his head. Aaron was surprised to see an expression of guilt wash over his face. Maybe he wasn't unreachable after all.

"Jacob?" Reuben prompted when his son didn't speak.

"It's nothing, Daed. Just a joke."

"Letting the horses loose wasn't a joke. Stealing a turkey and now a goat isn't a joke."

"Sure it is, Daed. Where's your sense of humor?"

Reuben shook his head. "You are hurting our friend Mahlon."

At the word *friend* attached to Mahlon's name, Aaron felt Jake go rigid. He glared at his father, all traces of remorse gone. "Friend?" he spat. "He is not my friend. You know he fired me!"

"But what did you do to him, Jake?"

"I didn't do anything to him! I was just working the horses, doing my job. *He* made a big deal out of nothing! He's the one you should be giving a hard time. *He's* the problem, not me."

Reuben didn't react to the venom or the misrepresentation. "He wants the best for you, Jacob."

Jake scoffed.

"Your father's right, Jake." Mahlon walked out of the darkness into the circle of light cast by the lantern. "I know you don't believe me, but I have only your good at heart."

"You're right about one thing. I don't believe you!" Jake tried to wrench himself from Aaron's grasp. "Let me go!"

Aaron tightened his grip on the shirt and wrapped an arm around Jake's waist. An elbow came flying back and clipped Aaron in the gut. He grunted and held Jake closer.

"We all want the best for you, Jake." Another man stepped out of the shadows. Aaron recognized him from church. It was the bishop.

When Jake saw him, he redoubled his efforts to get free, elbows flying, feet kicking. Aaron grabbed Jake's arms and pinned them behind him, then forced him to kneel.

"You have to stop this wild life, Jake, before you get hurt or you hurt someone else." Three other men appeared, Jake's older brothers, and it was the oldest who had spoken.

"I don't believe it." Scorn blistered Jake's words. "Is Mamm coming next?"

"'Honor thy father and mother,' which is the first commandment with a promise: 'That it may be well with thee, and thou mayest live long on the earth,'" quoted the bishop.

"What are you going to do to me if I don't?" Jake sneered. "You can't make me do something I don't want to do."

Aaron thought Jake had a point. There came a time when a son or daughter who chose to rebel was beyond both instruction and punishment. They became too stubborn and bent on their own way to be reached, and only the consequences of their actions would teach them.

"We don't want to make you do anything, Jacob." Reuben reached a hand toward his boy. "All we want is for you to lose your anger and live right."

With a colossal effort, Jake wrenched an arm free and batted his father's hand away. There were gasps all around, but it was the grief on Reuben's face that hurt Aaron.

Aaron resecured the arm, resolved not to let Jake surprise him again.

"Please, Jake," Reuben begged. "Stop this terrible behavior. I beg you."

Jake glared at his father and let loose a cruel, sarcastic laugh.

Reuben sighed. "Let him go, Aaron."

"Are you sure?" Aaron had no doubt that the man would bolt. He suspected Reuben knew that too.

"I am sure. He must choose to remain, or everything we try is in vain."

"Fat chance of that happening." Jake twisted free as Aaron dropped his arms. He spun quickly and his fist flashed. Aaron had expected an attack and was ready. He blocked the punch and hit Jake in the gut none too gently, but without the deliberate power and none of the anger coiled in Jake.

Not having expected any retaliation, Jake's eyes went wide as the wind was knocked out of him. He gasped, bent double, and grabbed his middle.

Behind Jake, five Amish men stared at Aaron in disbelief.

Aaron tried to reassure them. "He's not hurt, just winded. I apologize if I offended you. Sometimes I have difficulty turning the other cheek."

"I'll get you for this," Jake hissed when he had enough air to speak.

Aaron just raised an eyebrow. He doubted he'd ever see the man again. Jake was a coward who struck at night against those who couldn't or wouldn't strike back.

Jake sent a final glare at his father and ran. He jumped over the fence and tore down the lane.

Aaron and the others watched him disappear into the night.

"He limps," Reuben observed, looking at Aaron in question.

"The goat kicked him."

"Ah. As you might say, a consequence. I hope he does not need many more of them to see the error of his ways."

The noise of a car door slamming and a car peeling out sounded clearly now that the animals were calming. Aaron shook his head. Jake had a friend waiting. He couldn't help wondering if the friend had ever considered the difficulty of having a goat in his car.

"I'm sorry, Reuben." The bishop put a hand on the man's shoulder.

Reuben nodded, but he seemed broken, a man in pain. His remaining sons gathered at his back, offering their support, and Mahlon stood at his side, silently offering strength and comfort.

Aaron watched these men—solid, good, responsible men. He was impressed by the way they stood with Reuben in his time of need. And he knew he was the outsider.

He left the compound, this time by the gate.

20

Aaron wandered back to his bedroom and sank onto his bed, pondering the events of the night. He admired men like Reuben Stoltzfus and Mahlon Eaby. They were fine men who lived what their faith taught. If it were up to him, he'd call the police and turn Jake in. He'd ask for a big, tough cop to find Jake and read him the riot act. Scare him straight.

But that wasn't the Amish way.

He fell back on his pillow and slept fitfully the rest of the night. Every time he awoke, he compared himself with Mahlon and the others, and he found himself wanting.

He was tired and more than slightly cranky all the next day, but he brightened a little in the late afternoon when he heard Trent's voice call, "Anyone here?"

Aaron, who was out in the pasture checking on the colt, returned to the barn to find Trent down on one knee, scratching a happy Missy. Another member of the Missy fan club. He stood when Aaron entered the room.

"Hey there." Aaron gestured to the blue silk shirt Trent had on. "Nice threads."

Trent grinned. "I like it."

"I should hope so. Whoever bought that has impeccable taste."

Trent shrugged. "Maybe he does. I haven't the vaguest idea."

The men walked to Aaron's room. Trent took the chair, and Aaron bunched the pillows behind his back as he leaned against the headboard.

"We caught Jake in the act last night." Aaron shook his head at the memory and told the story. "I was surprised when Reuben, the bishop, the Stoltzfus brothers, and Mahlon appeared. Apparently they all thought Jake would try something again because he had come home after being gone a few days, and he was still ranting about Mahlon. When he snuck out last night, Reuben and his sons followed. The bishop was already here, waiting with Mahlon."

"And you didn't know their plan?"

"I didn't. I ran out when I heard the chaos, thinking it might be a fox."

"You actually socked Jake in the stomach?" Trent seemed amazed.

"Not hard, though he definitely could do with a more solid one." He gave his friend a small, rueful smile. "I'm not a good Amish man."

Trent shook his head. "Not so. You've done just fine as far as I can see."

"By biting my tongue a lot."

"No one challenged you, did they? Does anyone suspect?"

"Everyone's been nothing but kind, and I don't think anyone knows, but it's time to stop."

"Only one more day."

"That was our agreement," Aaron said. "But as soon as the auction is finished, our experiment has to be over. I'm ready to have my life and my name back."

Trent nodded. "Me too. Your family comes home tomorrow, don't they? So I'll need to move out."

"They do. I want to be there to hear my sisters spin their tales." He grinned just thinking about them. Olivia would tell him about every activity, turning them all into exciting or humorous adventures, and she'd throw her hands about wildly in her enthusiasm. Victoria would listen and try to believe she'd been on the same trip since she would tell of all the difficulties and disappointments. The truth of the trip would lie somewhere in the middle, probably in his mother's version.

Trent held out a large envelope. "By the way, this came for you."

Aaron's heart stuttered. He took the envelope, his hands shaking more than a little bit. The return address read, *Division of Family Medicine, Duke University School of Medicine.* He took a deep breath. This was it. His future.

Lord, give me the grace to accept the answer, whatever it is.

He slid his finger under the flap, breaking the seal. He opened the envelope and pulled out the papers inside. Taking another bracing breath, he began to read.

Welcome to the Duke Family Medicine Residency Program, Dr. Ingleston.

He felt tears prick and knew it was a good thing he was sitting on the bed because his knees went weak with relief and joy.

"It's good?" his friend asked.

"It's more than good. It's excellent. Couldn't be better, at least from my point of view. What my father will think is another thing entirely. He doesn't know I applied for this transfer because I didn't tell him. He only knows I'm thinking about doing it. He still thinks he can talk me out of it. He probably spent his whole vacation honing his reasons why his choice for me is right."

"How will he take the news?" Trent indicated the letter.

"I don't really know. I know he won't be happy, but he also won't do anything drastic like shun me."

"Of course not. You're English."

"I'm hoping he will recognize a done deal and try to be pleased for me."

"And if he doesn't? If he isn't?"

Aaron readjusted his pillows. "This time on the farm in a different world from the one I know has helped me see that sometimes a choice is between better and best, not good and evil. Good and evil are absolutes, but better and best can differ, depending on your point of view. I think best would be to call the police on Jake. Mahlon and the others think best is the community handling him. Varying views but with the same goal—saving Jake."

"So your dad thinks you and he being partners, surgeons together, is best."

"And I think my becoming a family physician is best."

"Two views of how to arrive at one conclusion—you, a happy and productive doctor."

Aaron reread the letter. He couldn't stop smiling.

Trent had to laugh. "Your father should see your expression right now. He'd recognize that you know what you're doing."

Aaron dropped his legs over the side of the bed and put his elbows on his knees. He leaned forward. "What about you? These two weeks have been for you too."

Trent sat forward, his pose a mirror of Aaron's. "It's been good. I've learned a lot about myself."

"And? Do you want to go back to being Amish? Did living English for a while help you reach any decisions?"

Trent ran a hand over his jeans. "You know, these jeans are comfortable enough and a mark of English culture if anything is, but I like my old black pants better."

Aaron laughed as he admired his own black pants. "They are roomier."

"Easier to move in, more comfortable, and sturdier."

"A great reason to remain Amish if I ever heard one."

"Ha! I know sarcasm when I hear it."

"You must have been corrupted by the world."

"I was afraid I would be too weak or frightened by the English world to manage there, no matter how much I wanted to try it. After these two weeks, I know I could live English. It would be lonely and hard, especially at first, but I could do it."

"That's a good thing to learn about yourself. It helps you make a decision from strength, not fear."

"I also realized that fear isn't a good reason to stay Amish. I don't want to be scared into what I believe."

"So why would you remain Amish?"

"Sally. I know I don't have a chance with her if I become English."

"That's probably right, but is a girl, even one as nice and kind and pretty as Sally, a good reason to choose how to spend your life? Will you choose her and end up resenting her because she kept you from the freedoms you craved?"

"Those are good questions. I can't put the burden of my choice on her. I know how my father can make me feel with his badgering me to be a good Amish man. I don't think Sally would ever badger anyone, but I'd know what she wanted and expected from me. It would break my heart if I came to resent her like I resent my dad."

"So why else would you remain Amish?"

Trent considered. "Last Sunday I drove by here a couple of times, watching everyone go to church. The men all wore their white shirts and black vests, the women their black dresses, and the single girls like Sally the blue dresses with the white aprons. They were saying by their similar dress that they submitted to the community. If I stay Amish, it can only be because I'm willing to submit too. And I would submit if I decide that's where I'm nourished. It's where I'm strengthened and built up in my faith. If I remain Amish, it's got to be because I believe commitment to the Ordnung and Gott is the best way to live. I must believe that way of life is to help me and grow me, not limit me."

"In other words, you remain Amish because you know it's best for you, not because your father wants you to."

He nodded. "I'm almost persuaded."

Aaron stood, putting the envelope and letter on his bureau. "Like the king in the Bible."

"I've always wondered if, on one day that's not recorded, he chose Christianity."

"Well, tomorrow's Saturday, the auction, and the day my family comes home. You don't have to decide by then, but you do have to move out and I have to move in."

Trent made a face. "It's going to be awkward, explaining to Mahlon."

"I feel foolish that I never anticipated how deceptive we would look. How deceptive we've been. The fact that that wasn't our intention doesn't change the fact that we've lied. Do you feel as guilty as I do?"

"Maybe more so, especially about Sally and Aubrey. Who would have thought in this short time we'd both meet women who interested us so much? I hated lying to them."

"So did I," Aaron said. "But it's not like we could tell them earlier. We couldn't ask them to lie for us, and we still needed our answers."

"That's true. All we were thinking was how to find out whether we truly agreed with our fathers. That's what started this whole charade."

Aaron leaned against the door frame. "And we're the ones who have to stop it."

"Tomorrow. After the auction. Until then, I'm still English and you're still Amish."

Aaron thought of Aubrey sharing her hurtful experience with Ethan, trusting him with her pain. His gut twisted when he thought of her reaction to his deceit. He sighed. "I can't help feeling the sky's about to fall on us."

When Aubrey finished her session with Miriam and Mahlon late Friday afternoon, she came outside and found that Trent had brought his family pickup truck. She laughed. "Quite a change from that lovely convertible."

"They use it to pull the horse trailer to competitions," Aaron said.

"And you know this how?" she teased.

"Uh . . ." He swallowed visibly.

Trent jumped in. "I was just telling him about it."

She smiled at Trent. "Well, it's great you have something like that for the larger things Mahlon is sending."

The men packed narrow wooden shelves Mahlon had made before the accident. "Those are for cooking spices. I made some for Miriam when we were first married, and she says they help keep the kitchen organized. She's the one who suggested I make some for the auction this year."

Aubrey smiled at the explanation. For Mahlon, things needed to have a purpose, and often that purpose was making his wife happy. His devotion was touching.

The guys carefully placed a gorgeous rocking chair in the truck. Aaron ran his hand over the silky-smooth wood. "This is a thing of beauty, Mahlon."

Mahlon gave a modest smile. "It's how I pass the winter. It gives me pleasure, and the things I make are good and useful things. Working with my hands is another way to glorify Gott. After all, everything is the work of His hands."

There were also unexpected treasures to go in the pickup: a large cooler, a selection of essential oils, a pair of pillows Miriam had made that could be heated and placed on sore muscles, and a ten-dollar coupon for the Amish shoe store. It would be interesting to see how much beyond their original sale price these auction items would garner for the children's home.

Trent had brought along his own contributions to the occasion—pots of Shasta daisies and black-eyed Susans as well as hostas and mums.

"Pretty flowers." Aaron fingered the petals, then raised an eyebrow at Trent. "From your garden?"

Trent colored. "It needed thinning."

"Right." He patted Trent on the back.

Mahlon stood on the porch and supervised the preparations. "Here's the safety vest for you, Aaron," he called, holding out the acid-green garment with FIRE POLICE in capital letters across the back.

Aubrey took it from him. "Why don't I keep it in my car so it doesn't get misplaced?"

Aaron braced the rocking chair with the cooler. "Thanks, Aubrey."

"And don't forget the traffic cones," Mahlon called again.

Aaron paused in the act of packing quilts around the chair to protect it on its journey. "Got them loaded already."

Trent climbed into the driver's seat. "Come on, Aaron. Let's get this stuff delivered."

"Going someplace important?"

"It's Friday night. Excellent television shows."

Aaron glanced in Trent's direction. "You could easily become a TV addict."

"I'm afraid I could."

Aaron chuckled. "All right, we're almost finished. Did we forget anything, Mahlon?"

"Your hat." Mahlon pointed to his head.

Aaron reached up. Sure enough—no hat. "It's in my room."

"I'll get it," Aubrey offered. "Finish securing that chair."

Aaron smiled at her, a pair of bungee cords dangling from his hand. "Thanks. It's hanging on the hook by the door."

She hurried into the barn and to Aaron's room. She felt awkward entering, but it was quick in, grab the hat, quick out. That was all.

She stepped in and almost slipped on a paper that had fallen to the floor. A breeze from the open window picked it up, then it settled again. She picked it up and couldn't help seeing the letterhead. *Duke University School of Medicine, Division of Family Medicine.* The word *Welcome* leaped out at her.

Trent was going to Duke! Good for him. That meant South Carolina, if she remembered correctly. Or maybe North Carolina. She always got those two states confused. Not geographically, but what towns and cities were in which state.

Almost immediately another thought occurred. *Poor Sally.*

Not that there had ever been a real chance for that relationship to begin with. Amish Sally and English Trent? It'd never work. Like Amish Aaron and English Aubrey. She stared blindly at the letter. *Amish Aaron and English Aubrey.* What was wrong with her that she fell for guys who never worked out? First Ethan and now Aaron. At least she had better taste with Aaron. He was a good man, an honorable man. An impossible man, but a man worth her heart.

With a sigh, she put the letter on top of a manila envelope resting on the bureau and ran out with Aaron's hat. She handed it to him.

He gave her that charming smile as he took it. "Don't forget I need to talk with you. It's important."

"Now?"

"Not now." Trent revved the engine. "We have to get this stuff to the auction site so I can get home."

Aaron rolled his eyes.

"Besides," Trent added, "you need time and privacy."

Time and privacy? What did that mean?

"That's true," Aaron agreed. "Tomorrow after the auction?"

"Tomorrow."

21

Early Saturday morning, Aubrey pulled into the Eabys' lane. Sally and Miriam were waiting for her with wonderful offerings for the auction food tent. There were fried apple pies and whoopie pies, pickled eggs and pickled beets, shoofly pies, and pumpkin pies made with pumpkins Miriam had grown, harvested, and put up last fall. There were large containers full of cut fruit and several gallons of milk packed in ice-filled coolers, all for the smoothies Sally would be making. There were also four electric blenders to make the smoothies in.

How did they do it all? It was just further proof that Aubrey could never be Amish, could never make a proper wife for Aaron.

There was no time for moping. She shook off her gloom and jumped in to help the women.

Aubrey arrived at the auction site around seven o'clock with Sally as her passenger. She pulled into a farm lane that separated two large fields. The one to the right was the parking area, and though the auction wasn't supposed to open until eight, there were a few cars and several buggies already there. The horses were in a pasture behind a barn at the end of the lane.

In the field to the left, two large tents had been erected, and a number of people rushed around with last-minute things to do. She pulled in and parked where a teenage boy pointed. She and Sally unloaded their supplies and made their way to the food tent.

"Oh my!" Aubrey looked down the center aisle at all the tables and all the goodies. It smelled like a combination of bakery and candy shop. The Amish did like their sugar.

When she carried the blenders to the table assigned to Sally and her coworkers, she found Trent working on connecting the electricity to a generator via a network of extension cords. Trent was sweating as he worked, his face red and his shoulders tense.

"I'd help," she said, "but all I know about electricity is that I like it a lot. But shouldn't you make sure that plug isn't in that puddle?" She pointed to a connection that lay in a depression still filled with water from a rain shower two days ago.

"Good observation." His smile of thanks was more a grimace from the effort he was putting in.

It was impressive to see an English man with so little fear of physical labor. *Aaron must be rubbing off on him.*

"Hey, Aubrey, Sally." Aaron walked up and bent over Trent. "How's the hookup coming?" He pointed to the puddle. "Let's move everything about a foot to the left to avoid electrocuting anyone."

Trent grinned. "Aubrey just said the same thing."

Aaron slid a glance her way, eyebrow raised. "Did she now?"

"She did," Aubrey said, and grinned at him.

He secured the various cords with duct tape and made sure all the blenders were plugged in. "You're ready to go, Sally."

Aubrey studied Aaron. He was an amazing man. Not only was he handsome, but he knew something about everything, yet remained kind and humble. She admired him way too much. He made her stomach flutter and her blood fizz. And he made her want to cry as she remembered the impossibility of a relationship.

Before he realized she was eyeing him, she blinked away threatening tears and forced herself to watch a pair of men setting up a grill that, according to a sign hanging on the pole, would be cooking grilled sausages and burgers, fifty cents each.

Aaron walked to her. "I've got a few minutes before I have to throw myself into weekend traffic on a highway. Want to walk around and see everything?"

Aubrey grinned. Of course she did. They took a stroll around the grounds, chatting. Aaron seemed tense. Surely he wasn't nervous about directing traffic? In much too short a time, she was watching him put on his green safety vest and take his place in the middle of the road. Buggies started arriving by the score, and cars slowed as they passed, not just because of all the buggy traffic but to gawk at all the activity. Aaron and his young assistants kept everything moving smoothly.

Aubrey wandered off to look around some more. If she was being honest, she had to admit she hadn't noticed much but Aaron when she walked around with him. When she considered Ethan and Aaron, she couldn't imagine what she'd ever seen in Ethan. He had been vain and manipulative, while Aaron was so honest and trustworthy. A thief versus an honorable man—there was no comparison.

Aubrey stood outside the back of the auction tent, which had its sides rolled up in the warm sun. It was only about a quarter full this early in the day, mostly with women sitting in clusters in the many rows of chairs. Simon, the auctioneer, stood on a platform and was already going at full steam. Just as Sally had said, he was amazing. Aubrey had to laugh as he auctioned off a three-book series by a well-known writer of Amish novels. An Amish woman seemed excited to win them. Whether she planned to read them or keep them out of circulation was anyone's guess.

Then came the large cooler Aaron and Trent had brought last night. Simon had three men who assisted him by standing at intervals facing the bidders. They kept track of who bid and in what order by pointing as each bidder raised a hand. The blue-and-white chest went to a woman who seemed overjoyed with her acquisition in spite of the outlandish price she was paying.

As she wandered around, Aubrey realized this auction was definitely an Amish event. There were very few English here, and there was little of the English language heard.

She went to Sally's table, where she and two of her sisters were working.

"Blueberries, strawberries, and bananas, please," Aubrey said to them.

"Extra fruit for a friend." Sally dumped substantial amounts into the blender and added fresh milk from a gallon jug. While the blender whirled, Aubrey checked to see that the cords were still well away from the puddle. They were.

She paid for her smoothie and wandered about as she drank. Everywhere she saw evidence of great organizational skills on someone's part. The scope of the event was amazing. The different-style Kapps, aprons, and capes on the women showed the geographical breadth of the attendees.

As she wandered past the auction tent, she noticed a section off to the side she hadn't seen before. It was filled with piles of lovely quilts and the most beautiful pieces of woodwork. A dining set consisting of a table and four chairs sat next to Mahlon's wonderful rocking chair. A book chest sat beside a bedroom set. An end table sat beside half a dozen footstools. The wood seemed to gleam in the early morning light, and Aubrey paused to run her fingers over a particularly well-worked piece of oak, marveling at its smoothness and warmth. She moved on to the quilts and lost herself for several minutes among the vivid colors and perfectly executed patterns. She could only imagine how cozy one of these would be on her bed in the dead of winter. She would never cease to be amazed by the talent and hard work of these people.

As she glanced at the half-filled auction tent, she realized these items were being saved for later in the day when the crowds would be larger. Again someone had thought carefully about the pacing of the day.

She should leave. She certainly didn't have money to bid on anything. A flurry of activity from the food tent caught her attention.

"Help!" someone cried, the voice shrill with fear. "Someone help us!"

People rushed toward the crisis, and Aubrey joined them. She was a physical therapist, not a nurse or doctor, but perhaps she could help, or find help if needed.

"Mamm!" a woman cried, and Aubrey saw her disappear as she presumably fell to her knees beside whoever had collapsed.

"What happened?"

"Who's sick?"

"Can anyone help?"

Aubrey pulled out her phone and called 911. The dispatcher promised to send an ambulance right away.

She hung up and cast about for Trent. He was going to Duke for a residency program. That meant he'd already graduated from med school. He'd know what to do. "Trent! Trent!"

She spotted him and pushed her way through the crowd. She interrupted his conversation with an Amish man in a straw hat with a different brim than the flat ones she was used to.

"Someone's sick or hurt. You've got to help whoever it is." She pointed to the food tent.

His face registered concern. "What happened?"

"I don't know. I just heard cries for help. Please hurry."

He nodded and wove through the crowd toward the tent. Aubrey still couldn't see what was going on through the throng of intervening people. She did see Trent reach the circle of people. He dropped down, disappearing from her view.

Almost instantly he popped up again and began pushing his way through the crowd, away from the person in trouble. To her great surprise he disappeared toward the parking area. She stared after him. What was that all about?

Almost immediately he reappeared with Aaron. As they ran toward the food tent, Trent talked to Aaron, who listened intently.

They disappeared into the crowd. She lost sight of them, though she could follow their progress by the movement of the people stepping aside for them. It appeared that those surrounding the fallen woman moved back slightly when the two arrived.

Sirens sounded, coming closer and closer. Her 911 call had borne fruit. A police car and an ambulance pulled into the lane and came to a stop beside the auction tent, silencing Simon and scattering people as they came. The police quickly moved people back from the woman who had collapsed. The EMTs climbed from the ambulance and raced to care for the victim.

Suddenly Aubrey could see what was happening as the police pushed back the crowd. Trent and Aaron were on their knees beside the victim. It was impossible to tell from this distance what had happened, and she could hear people saying everything from "stroke" to "heart attack." She might not have the specifics, but it was clearly serious.

The EMTs joined Trent and Aaron around the woman. Aaron stayed on his knees, hands busy, and started talking to the new arrivals. The EMTs nodded. They were working together, but Aaron was clearly in charge.

One of the EMTs rose and went to their vehicle. He pulled a gurney out and quickly wheeled it into the food tent.

"On the count of three." Aaron's voice floated over the low murmurs of the crowd. "One, two, three."

The four men lifted an older woman and laid her on the gurney. An EMT strapped her down and the men pushed her to the ambulance. They loaded her, and then one of the EMTs climbed in with her, while the other ran to the driver's seat. With their lights flashing, they drove away.

An Amish woman stood beside Aaron, watching the retreating ambulance. *The ill woman's daughter?*

But that wasn't Aubrey's concern. She stared at Aaron's back as he watched the ambulance drive away. Pictures of the last two weeks flashed in a mental slide show.

Aaron checking her engine and changing her tire.

Aaron caring for Harper after her fall down the stairs.

Aaron saddling Peaceable.

Aaron having the letter from Duke in his room.

And now Aaron telling the EMTs what to do.

These were not things an Amish man would do. How could she have been so stupid a second time?

"Dr. Ingleston," she called. "Dr. Trent Ingleston!"

Without a second's hesitation, Aaron turned. "Yes?"

Their eyes met, and she knew. She'd been taken in again.

She turned away.

"Aubrey, wait!"

She stopped, back still to him. She couldn't wait to hear his excuses and explanation. And she'd thought him honorable!

He jogged to her. "Would you please take Huldah here to Lancaster General so she can be with her mother?"

Whatever she had expected him to say, that wasn't it.

"This is Aubrey, Huldah." He spoke to the Amish woman beside him. "She can drive you. Tell your family where you're going, and you can call them later with news about your mother." He held out a cell phone. "Can you reach someone by phone? Maybe they can join you."

"I have a phone I use for my jams and jelly business." She patted her purse. "My husband has one he uses for his construction business. I can reach him."

Aaron—make that Trent—nodded.

Huldah turned red-rimmed eyes to Aubrey. "Denke for your kindness. Just give me a minute." She hurried to a group of people huddled together by the food tent.

"Aubrey—" Trent began.

She held out a hand. "No."

In spite of all the activity around them, all she heard was the silence between them.

22

The real Aaron Ropp stood off to the side and watched the less-than-friendly exchange between Trent and Aubrey. That was *not* how he wanted things to go between him and Sally, though he'd been just as dishonest as Trent and probably deserved it. Yesterday he had told Trent that he could see himself living in the English world. While that was still true, he couldn't imagine turning his back on the traditions and faith he loved. He might as well admit it—he was Amish to his toes. He'd enjoyed his English vacation, but it was time to return home.

He turned toward the food tent. He needed to talk to Sally immediately. He needed to explain to her why he and Trent had exchanged identities. One thing he knew for sure—they had never intended or expected to hurt anyone. He hoped that would be enough.

He found her at the smoothie table. "Sally, I need to talk to you. Can you get away for a few minutes?"

"Now?" Sally paused in the middle of scooping raspberries into a blender.

"I'm sorry. I know you're busy, but it's important."

She looked at the two young women with her, sisters probably. They all had the same crinkly-eyed smile, though Sally's was by far the warmest.

"Go ahead, Sally," said one. "We'll be fine for a little while. Just be back before lunchtime."

They walked through the crowds around the tents and over to the area where the buggies were parked. Here things were quiet and they could talk uninterrupted, but they were still visible to any interested eyes. The calm was restful after the excitement at the tents.

"Did you see that woman who collapsed?" Sally asked. "Did you help her?"

"You couldn't see what was going on?"

"Too many people, even though I wasn't all that far away. I heard someone say some doctor was here and helped. I figured that was you."

Aaron sighed. "I'm not a doctor, Sally. That's what I want to talk to you about."

She tilted her head in question.

Where to start? Might as well try the beginning. "I grew up in Iowa."

"Iowa? I thought you came from Honey Brook."

He shook his head. "Iowa. In a very conservative Amish community."

"You were Amish?"

"I *am* Amish."

She took a step back, coming up against the gray side of a buggy. "No. You can't be Amish. Look at your clothes, your car."

"They're not mine. They're Trent's."

She frowned, thoroughly confused. "You're Trent."

"No. I'm Aaron Ropp."

She stared at him for a minute, eyes narrowed, disbelief and a hint of anger replacing the smile he so loved. "Then what are you doing making believe you're Trent?"

"When I came to help Mahlon—"

"Wait a minute. Does Mahlon know you're not Trent?"

He wished she wouldn't interrupt, but she had hit on another point of guilt. "No, not yet. But I'm going to tell him."

"How are you going to explain it?" Each word struck sharp as a buggy whip.

Aaron put up a hand. "I don't know. Let me just explain to you right now."

She studied him, emotions flitting across her face. The anger was still there, tempered by a touch of sadness and—relief? He didn't understand that one, and this was the wrong time to analyze it. He had to complete his confession.

"I was walking along the road on the last leg of my journey from Iowa when Trent pulled up and offered me a ride." He told her about their lunch and their conversation. And Trent's idea.

"'Why don't we trade places for a couple of weeks?' he said. At first I thought he was crazy, but the more he talked, the better the idea seemed. 'I can do something completely different and unscramble my brains after my confrontation with my father, and you can see if being English is what you want. Win-win.' I was struggling with whether to be baptized, and he presented me with the idea of trying English life out for a time so I could make a wise choice. It seemed just what I needed."

"But you deceived people. You deceived *me*."

No sugarcoating it with Sally. She went right to the main issue. He dared to think that a future life with her would be interesting. A good woman who would keep him honest was just what he needed. If she'd ever have him now. He went cold as he thought about how she must view him.

"We did deceive people," he agreed. "And that was wrong. We never even considered that part of what we were doing. We figured Mahlon would still get the help he needed, it was only for two weeks, and it was a way for both of us to find out what we wanted." He gazed at her. "I certainly didn't think I'd meet you."

She glared at him. "You put me through a terrible time."

"Really?" He felt a surge of hope.

"And you still might. What have you decided about leaving? I cannot become involved with an English man. I promised Gott."

She'd talked to Gott about him? That sounded promising. "Like I said, I come from a very conservative community. As I've come to understand during these past two weeks, it was the conservatism of my community that bothered me, not Amish life itself. I've watched Mahlon and Miriam and studied the local people, and there's enough room here for me to breathe. As I watch everyone here today, I realize *these* are my people, unlike the people I see on TV at Trent's. I think like an Amish man, I *am* an Amish man, and I don't want to change."

She softened for a split second. Then she crossed her arms and said, "You must prove it, you know."

"I know. I must go and ask Mahlon's forgiveness. While I didn't mean harm with the deceit, I must acknowledge it for what it is. And I ask your forgiveness. From the first time I saw you smile, I thought how easy it would be to choose to stay because of you."

Her eyes widened in alarm.

"But that's not why I made the decision," he said quickly. "I have based it on my commitment to Gott and our community."

She relaxed.

He peered into her face. "Forgive me?"

Her silence was agonizing. How long would she make him wait for an answer?

Finally, she said, "Gott has forgiven me and asks me to forgive others. I forgive your deceit."

He smiled at her, touched by her kindness and good heart. "I will prove myself to you. You will see."

"I hope so, Aaron. I hope so."

Sunday night Aubrey sat in her apartment, bent double as she rested her forehead on Buster's soft fur. Sensory comfort.

"I did it again, baby. I trusted a deceitful man."

Buster twisted until he could kiss her cheek.

"Why can't I find a man as faithful and honest as you, sweet boy?"

She sat up, pulling him with her until he was cradled in her arms. She buried her face in his soft neck and blinked back tears. She'd cried enough over men. *No more.* She punched the sofa cushion for emphasis, making Buster raise his head in confusion.

"Sorry, baby."

He licked her cheek again and settled back into her arms.

The depths of her hurt irritated her. She'd only known him for two weeks. Why should his deception affect her so deeply? Had she felt this devastation over Ethan?

A knock sounded on her apartment door. Buster abandoned his role as comforter and went into protector mode. He raced to the door, barking fiercely.

"Good boy." Aubrey walked to the door and peered through the peephole. She gasped. "It's him!" she hissed at Buster, who stopped barking to stare at her absurd behavior.

The knock sounded again.

She stepped away from the door and straightened. She could do this. She could and would face him down. She opened the door, scowl in place to cover the hurt.

Aaron—no, *Trent* stood there. He had no business looking that good in jeans and a T-shirt, especially when she was so angry with him. "May I come in? We need to talk."

"*You* may need to talk, but what makes you think I want to listen?" She turned and stalked into the apartment.

He hesitated a moment but seemed to take the open door as an invitation of sorts. He followed her in and shut the door.

Buster sat in the middle of the little entry hall and stared up at him. Aubrey knew he wasn't trying to block Trent. He was just doing his doggy-get-in-the-middle-of-everything thing.

Trent bent. "Hello there, boy. What's your name?" He held out his hand.

That was all the prompting Buster needed. He threw himself at Trent, licking the man's face with his tail going a mile a minute.

"That's Buster." She couldn't imagine what she'd have done without her dog this past year.

After giving the dog a good scratch, Trent straightened. "He likes me. Dogs are good judges of character, you know."

"Ha! He thought Ethan was wonderful too."

"Okay. That puts me in my place." He stood uncertainly in the middle of the living room.

"Oh, for heaven's sake, sit down." She indicated the comfy chair.

She sat in the corner of the sofa with her legs tucked under her. She stared at him, daring him to talk.

"I'm sorry," he said. "I never meant to hurt anyone."

"Mmm." She wished he didn't seem so sincere. It was easier to be angry when he was the bad guy. And angry was easier than hurt.

"It seemed like a good idea at the time." He stared off as if seeing the scene where the idea originated. "I'd picked up Aaron, and we were talking about our fathers and the pressure we were under." He gave her the whole story.

She listened to him talk, shutting her eyes for a moment. Maybe blocking him out visually would stop the ridiculous pattering of her heart. This guy hadn't stolen money, but he was a con man just the same.

"All I considered was that this was an opportunity for me to get my head together about my father, and a chance for Aaron to experience English life—"

"How thoughtful of you."

He barely flinched. "I needed time to decompress and plan my future."

Don't be so snide, Aubrey! Be nice. She would kill him with kindness. "So did your plan work?"

He sat back with a wry smile. "Aaron decided he wanted to remain Amish, but here in Honey Brook where it's less conservative. And yes, I was prepared to face my father."

"How did that conversation go?"

"Not as bad as I expected. Not as well as I hoped. He listened without interrupting and he read my letter from Duke without sneering. When he finished reading, he handed it back. 'I'm disappointed,' he said. 'I think you're wasting your gift. But good luck.'

"That was harsh."

He shrugged. "Maybe, but so much better than before. I think my mother spent their whole vacation talking to him, and he actually heard her. He'll eventually be fine because he does want all of us kids to be happy. He's just used to defining what *happy* means."

"Maybe your sisters will have more freedom to make their choices because of your stand."

"Maybe. I hope so."

They stared at each other across the small space between the chair and sofa, but it was the emotional chasm that loomed. She feared they might not be able to find a way across. Buster broke the awkwardness by jumping onto the sofa and lying down with his head in Aubrey's lap. She began to pet him. "So what now?"

Trent leaned forward, suddenly intense. "I've been thinking about what I wanted to say for so long. I have three things that I hope will help you understand."

She wanted to understand. She needed to know if he and Aaron had just made an unusually poor choice. She didn't know how she'd cope if it was a deeper issue of poor character.

"First, this switch was only for two weeks. I had spent the day thinking about my family's vacation, and that was the context of the idea. Two weeks. An English vacation on an Amish farm. An Amish vacation in an English house."

"Okay," she said dubiously.

"Second, Mahlon wasn't going to suffer. He was going to have someone to work with his horses. He didn't know either Aaron or me. I've grown up around horses just like he did, so what did it matter which one of us showed up?" He twisted his hands in anxiety. "I didn't think ahead about how we'd explain this to him after the two weeks were up, and neither did Aaron."

"Quite a little complication there."

He dipped his head in acknowledgement. "I went out to see him this afternoon. Aaron had already talked to him last night."

"And?"

"He was a little miffed, but after my help with Jake and Peaceable, he was inclined to forgive me."

"Yeah, you were the white knight to the rescue there."

He got up from the chair and moved to the sofa, his back against the far arm. Buster, curled between them, glanced at him, then got up and rearranged himself with his head on Trent's knee. Trent began running his hand down the dog's back. Buster sighed with contentment.

Aubrey studied the pair bonding before her eyes. She wanted to trust Trent so badly.

"Then there is the third and most important issue—you." He watched her, his expression intense.

Her heart skipped.

"The last thing I expected was to meet you. Yet there you were, kind, smart, beautiful, and needing my help with your car. There I was in broadfall pants and a straw hat. It never occurred to me that during our two weeks of switching roles I'd meet a girl who seems to be everything I didn't even realize I needed."

The prayer came automatically. *Oh, God, what should I do?*

"Remember how I asked to speak with you a couple of times? I wanted to tell you who I really was before you discovered it accidentally, which of course is what happened. And it made me seem sneakier than I am. I promise you, I'm not a guy who makes a habit of tricking people." He looked her straight in the eye. "I'm not Ethan."

She closed her eyes and searched for the answer to her prayer.

And she knew.

"Can we start again?" she said. "Get to know each other honestly? You need to show me who you really are, and I need to discover if what you've said about yourself is true."

His face broke into a broad grin. "Yes please. It's more than I deserve, so thank you."

She relaxed for the first time since he'd arrived.

"A lot of our getting to know each other will have to be online," he said. "I leave for Duke next week. But maybe you can come down for a weekend after I get settled? There's a hotel nearby."

"We'll see." But her heart was full of hope.

23

Aubrey beamed out the window at the rows of white chairs and the arched trellis covered with white tulle and pink and yellow roses. A lovely setting for a wedding.

Her wedding.

She stood still as her mother finished buttoning the tiny buttons that ran down the back of her gown. She couldn't stop smiling as her future mother-in-law and her mom arranged her veil carefully over her hair. Aubrey was going to be Mrs. Trent Ingleston, and they were being married in the Inglestons' beautiful backyard.

"Time for us to go," Mom whispered as she passed Aubrey her bouquet. "Love you, Aubrey. Be happy."

Aubrey kissed her mother, then Mrs. Ingleston. She hugged Olivia and Victoria, pretty in pink as her attendants. The twins had welcomed her into their family with open arms and their contagious high spirits, and their parents made her feel like one of their own.

They all slipped out of the room to give her a few moments to herself, and she gazed out the back window at the guests filling the seats outside.

"Small," she and Trent had kept saying as plans for the wedding swirled around them. "We'll have enough debt with schooling. We don't want more from a big wedding. And the wedding itself isn't that important anyway. It's the marriage that matters to us."

Through a diligent cutting of guest lists and lots of work making their own decorations—with the help of their Amish friends, of course—they managed to keep things under control. Aaron even managed to cut them a deal on the flowers. He'd wanted to do them for free, but Trent, ever honorable, wouldn't hear of it.

At first after he went off to Duke, Trent just wrote. And wrote. His correspondence revealed a man who loved God, had good character, and was trustworthy. Then she visited him and saw what his life was—long hours and hard work. She also saw that he loved what he was doing. When he finally proposed, he'd barely finished the question before she was emphatically agreeing.

They decided it was important to wait at least a year before marrying. Any questions about Trent's character had to be laid to rest, and time was the only way for that to happen. Now the year was up, and she had never felt happier.

Besides, that time had been necessary to find a house with a stable and pasture that they could move into after the wedding. After all, they needed someplace to keep Peaceable. "It's not right for the two of you to be apart," Mahlon told Trent when the young doctor had tried to argue. "I've never seen a horse so bonded to a person before. He'll let other people ride him, but it's plain as day he's only happy with you."

Peaceable had whinnied his agreement.

From her window vantage point she saw Sally and Aaron walk into the yard, Mahlon and Miriam behind them. Ben and Asa walked solemnly, while little Mahlon tried to mimic their seriousness. Anna and Harper danced along, holding their parents' hands and staring around wide-eyed at a world so different from theirs. Joseph clung to Harper's other hand, and a bright-eyed Naomi gazed around from her father's arms.

Aubrey gasped and peered closer at Miriam. She was expecting again!

Sally and Aaron had married last November, and Sally was due to give birth to their first child just before Christmas. She had positively glowed when she shared the news with Aubrey, who hadn't been able to resist squealing and throwing her arms around her Amish friend. Aaron had been hired to help Mahlon part-time and also worked at the local nursery. His goal was to save and open his own nursery, using the skills he'd learned from his mother and his employer.

Mahlon walked to a seat without a limp, and Aubrey smiled to see him so well. Good physical therapy healed many ills. Poor Miriam still had residual concussion issues, mostly occasional short-term memory problems, but the headaches were gone, and she ran her home on her own. There was still hope for a full recovery.

Bekka walked into view wearing a sleek blue dress with ridiculously high sparkly heels. She held on to the arm of her latest beau, an out-of-time hippie named Bowie. Bekka had met him at a lecture on saving the earth.

Bekka had stayed at home for six months before she left, not quite the year Aubrey had recommended, but better than nothing. During that time she had tried to make her parents understand, with only limited success. She'd lost interest in the universe and supernovas and had broken up with Carter. Her current cause was whales, even though she'd never seen the ocean and definitely had never seen a whale. She was living with three other girls in a tiny messy apartment and studying for her GED. She planned to go to college and major in environmental sciences. Aubrey was sure that healing with her parents would come in time, and meanwhile, Bekka was finally comfortable in her own skin.

The real surprise from those memorable two weeks was Jake. After months with no word, he had suddenly shown up on his parents' stoop one day, a changed man. He had fallen in with a bad crowd and gotten in trouble one too many times for his tastes. The world had indeed taught him about consequences, and he was ready to put his parents' hearts at ease and rejoin the community. He'd found work at a local furniture shop, where his boss praised his tireless work ethic and friendly attitude. There was talk of Jake being promoted to manager soon. Aubrey had also heard that he was courting Sally's sister Rhoda. Her parents had been unsure about the match at first, but Jake was working just as hard to change their minds as he was in his new job. God was truly a God of miracles.

Aubrey watched through a window as Trent's mother was escorted down the aisle by Scott. Her brother seated Mrs. Ingleston, then hurried back up the aisle to walk Mom down the aisle. Their faces all reflected the joy in Aubrey's heart.

A knock sounded and Dad peered around the door. "It's time, sweetheart."

They walked downstairs and out the back door. The soloist finished her number and Olivia and Victoria headed down the aisle, heads held high.

"I like him, Aubrey," Dad said. "He's a good man."

Aubrey's eyes were fixed on that good man, who gave her that smile that had melted her heart since the day she met him. "Yes, he is."

She took her father's arm and stepped forward into her future.

YOUR FEEDBACK MEANS A LOT TO US!

Up to this point, we've been doing all the writing. Now it's *your* turn!

Tell us what you think about this book, the characters, the plot, or anything else you'd like to share with us about this series. We can't wait to hear from *you*!

Log on to give us your feedback at:
https://www.surveymonkey.com/r/HeartsOfAmish

Annie's FICTION

AMISH INN MYSTERIES™

Escape into the exciting stories of the Amish Inn Mysteries!

Meet Liz Eckardt and the lovable members of the Material Girls quilting group in their peaceful town of Pleasant Creek, Indiana. The scenery and serenity at the heart of Indiana's Amish country will envelop you as these women solve thrilling mysteries. You'll be charmed by the bonds of friendship and family that are strengthened by each new challenge, whether it's catching a crafty killer or making it back to the Olde Mansion Inn in time for coffee hour with friends.

Get your copy of the first book now by logging on to
AnniesFiction.com!

Learn more about Annie's fiction books at
AnniesFiction.com

We've designed the website especially for you!

Access your e-books and audiobooks* • Manage your account

Choose from these great series:

Amish Inn Mysteries	Hearts of Amish Country
Annie's Attic Mysteries	Inn at Magnolia Harbor
Annie's Museum of Mysteries	Irish Tearoom Mysteries
Annie's Mystery Quilt Stitch Along	Love in Lancaster County
Annie's Mysteries Unraveled	Love in Sandcastle Cove
Annie's Quilted Mysteries	Mistletoe Mysteries
Annie's Secrets of the Quilt	Mysteries of Aspen Falls
Annie's Sweet Intrigue	Rose Cottage Book Club
Antique Shop Mysteries	Secrets of the Castleton Manor Library
Chocolate Shoppe Mysteries	Scottish Bakehouse Mysteries
Creative Woman Mysteries	Under the Mistletoe
Hearts in Peril	Victorian Mansion Flower Shop Mysteries

THREE FORMATS FOR YOUR CONVENIENCE

HARDCOVER    E-BOOK    AUDIOBOOK*

*available in select series only

What are you waiting for? **Annie's** FICTION